A
PEARL
Among
PRINCES

A PEARL Among PRINCES

COLEEN MURTAGH PARATORE

Dial Books for Young Readers
an imprint of Penguin Group (USA) Inc.

DIAL BOOKS FOR YOUNG READERS
A division of Penguin Young Readers Group
Published by The Penguin Group
Penguin Group (USA) Inc., 375 Hudson Street, New York, NY 10014, U.S.A.

Penguin Group (Canada), 90 Eglinton Avenue East, Suite 700, Toronto, Ontario, Canada
M4P 2Y3 (a division of Pearson Penguin Canada Inc.) • Penguin Books Ltd, 80 Strand,
London WC2R 0RL, England • Penguin Ireland, 25 St. Stephen's Green, Dublin 2, Ireland
(a division of Penguin Books Ltd) • Penguin Group (Australia), 250 Camberwell Road,
Camberwell, Victoria 3124, Australia (a division of Pearson Australia Group Pty Ltd) •
Penguin Books India Pvt Ltd, 11 Community Centre, Panchsheel Park, New Delhi—110
017, India • Penguin Group (NZ), 67 Apollo Drive, Rosedale, North Shore 0632, New
Zealand (a division of Pearson New Zealand Ltd) • Penguin Books (South Africa) (Pty)
Ltd, 24 Sturdee Avenue, Rosebank, Johannesburg 2196, South Africa • Penguin Books
Ltd, Registered Offices: 80 Strand, London WC2R 0RL, England

The publisher does not have any control over and does not assume any respon-
sibility for author or third-party websites or their content.
Designed by Nancy R. Leo-Kelly
Text set in Dante MT
Printed in the U.S.A.
1 3 5 7 9 10 8 6 4 2

Library of Congress Cataloging-in-Publication Data
is available upon request

❖❖❖❖❖

To my wonderful brothers,
Kevin, Danny, Jerry,
and Michael Murtagh—every one a prince.

With love always,
Col

Chapters

A
PEARL
Among
PRINCES

Old Mother Goose when
She wanted to wander
Would ride through the air
On a very fine gander.

CHAPTER I

Gracepearl's Calling

Soon, Gracepearl, my girl, soon. Your time approaches, destiny calls.

My mother's strange words dance through my mind as I climb the stone steps of the old bell tower. "What time, Mother? What destiny? Oh, how I wish you were here."

When I reach the turret, the wind lifts my hair and I breathe in gusts of fresh salty sea air. Raising my spyglass, I turn the gold rim for a bird's view of the world.

There below is Miramore. Lush trees waving, red and yellow flowered fields, rows of thatched cottages; there's mine, my friends Lu's and Nuff's, the gardens and orchards, then a turn to the coal yard, the farms, sheep grazing, the rooster-vane atop Mackree's stable, *ohh*, a cry escapes, my heart still stinging . . . then up the bend to the forest, the dancing circle, my pine place of peace . . . then off in the distance, the flitting banners of the royal lodge, the dining hall where my father, Cook, toils preparing tomorrow evening's Welcome Banquet, then down now toward the beach, the trading stalls, the fishermen's sheds, the black-robed professors assembling in the stands, clusters of Miramores in their finest garb gathering excitedly to await the arrivals . . . the docks, the piers, and then the water, *ahh*, the water, always the water, a vast flat wild blue indigo seacake frosted with white capped waves.

Miramore is a paradise, but paradise is not enough. Where does all that water lead? What lies beyond that horizon?

I have been happy here, well provided for and lucky in the love of my father and friends, but this past year something has changed. I have changed.

Haunted by strange and confusing dreams, faces of people I do not recognize, I wake with a mounting anxiousness, an overwhelming sense that I must go to them. To where or for what reason I do not know. I feel sure, though, with the same certainty that Mother guides me from the heavens above, that the moon will rise tonight, and the sun tomorrow, there is something more than Miramore for me.

My life must have greater purpose than digging coal and peeling potatoes. There is a longing, a rising, a storm-surf pounding, foaming in my heart. I want something more meaningful, more useful . . . *more*. I am convinced my fate lies beyond this sea. But what will it be? *Who will I be?* And what of the people in the dreams? Who are they? Somehow I sense they need my help.

Your time is coming, Gracepearl, my girl. Mother's sweet strong voice sings inside me again. The wind strokes my cheek like the palm of a hand, the wild sea beckons, come. Come, Gracepearl, come away.

"But where?" I shout. "How? There is no way to leave."

The dotted-tail gull on the ledge *caw-caws* and the pigeons at my feet *coo* too. "Easy for you," I say to them. "You have wings!"

Old Mother Goose when she wanted to wander would ride through the air on a very nice gander. The familiar rhyme flits through my mind. The only way to leave the island is by boat. The only boats sturdy enough are the royal ships that come each summer, the ships that arrive today. By birth, all Miramores serve the Order here, as our ancestors have done before us. The sons of farmers become farmers, the daughters of seamstresses, seamstresses, the sons of fishermen, fishermen. By lineage I will garden or cook. I hate to cook.

However . . . there is a way, one way to leave the island.

Should one of the visiting princes arriving today choose a Miramore girl to marry, she could sail off with him. This is a very recent change. Much to the giddy delight of the Muffets, those goose-brained girls set on nothing but marriage, the Royal Order of Bark has decreed that the rules of royal matrimony be amended.

A prince now may marry any girl he so chooses, even a peasant Miramore girl.

I could be the first.

"Tell me, Mother, would it be wrong to marry a prince for his ship?"

I giggle. The gull squawks. Today it all begins.

This is the twenty-first day of June, the very birthday of a new summer, and for decades upon decades, centuries now, this is the day the royal boys come to study the charming arts. They stay until September. "Princes in training" they are. Lu nicknamed them the "PITs" when we were little and now she, Nuff, and I couldn't call them otherwise.

Most Miramore girls, especially those silly "Muffets" who work in the fabric mills and dress alike in pink shawls, dream of marrying a prince. The Muffets imagine a life of luxury—servants and gowns and baubles and balls—like they've read about in fairy tales. And now that the rule change makes the fairy tale actually possible, they've even gotten worse.

Me? I prefer true tales. I have never met a PIT who

impressed me. Too full of themselves they are, rude and arrogant, self-centered and smug.

Not one holds a candle to my Mackree. Mackree Byre, my life's best friend.

But Mackree is mine no longer. My throat clenches and my lips tremble at the thought of his beautiful face. I have loved Mackree since we were playmates, swimming free as fish in the warm shallow bay, climbing trees wild as monkeys, riding his ponies on the beach. When we were ten Mackree wrote "Purl Will U Maree Me?" with a stick in the sand on Heart's Day. I wrote my answer: "Yes." We wove each other callaberry crowns. He was king; I was queen, of the sea and forest too.

Mackree loved me then, he loves me still. I know for certain he does. *But why* . . . the tears come again . . . *why is he now so cruel?* He avoids me like a swarm of locusts. What did I do to lose his affection? Why does he scorn me so?

This past Heart's Day there was no bouquet of violets tied with a ragged string, his usual gift to me. And when I brought him my Heart's card and a sack of his favorite skipping stones, which I'd collected especially for him, he ignored the card and tossed off the sack. "I'm a child no more," he said.

Then, on May Day, Mackree broke off with me for good.

"Summer's coming," he said, "you'll be sixteen. You want to leave here, Pearl. You've made that plain. Do us both a favor, and be done with it. Go. It's time you said yes to one of those princes always flirtin' with ya each year. And it's time I found a girl content with Miramore."

Your time is coming, Gracepearl, my girl. Mother speaks to me again.

Your destiny awaits you, darling. Soon, you will choose.

Three wise men of Gotham
Went to sea in a bowl,
And if the bowl had been stronger,
This rhyme would be longer.

CHAPTER 2

The Ships Arrive

"Choose what?" I call out, but Mother does not answer. Her simple words confound but intrigue me. A foghorn bellows in the distance. I point my spyglass out to the water now, hoping to spot the ships.

The Jaspian Sea encircles the island, a mighty and masterful moat. On this warm morning after spring impishly sent one last goose-bump night to remember her by, the ever-present sheet of fog off shore hangs heavy as an ermine stole.

The PITs come from the twelve branches of the Royal Order of Bark, fewer and fewer of them each year as the mothballed monarchies fade into history books. "The days of kings are numbered," Nora Baker, the baker, says. "People are starvin'. Them gold crowns have lost their glory."

Each summer, I help Nora serve a meal to the captains who transport the princes here before they set off home again. These past few years I've heard the old seamen talking of the lands across the water, whole villages of people suffering, as the never-ending war wages on. Last summer, especially, they spoke of neighbors, good men and women, with no work to be found, no way to put food on their families' tables, forced out of their homes, as they cannot pay the tariffs, some begging for bread now, hungry.

"It's shameful," Nora said, raising her fist, then slamming it down on her chopping block. "A disgrace, 'tis. Them royals oughtta sell them castles and spread the coins round."

Nora Baker and I don't often agree, but on that note we were rock solid.

I move my spyglass to my left eye to give my right a rest.

There, now, the tip of a ship nudges out of the mist, a sharp black nose on a white fog face. "Yes!" I shout to the pigeons and gull. "The first one has arrived."

I scan the sea searching for others. How many will come this year?

Last summer there were only nine princes in training, a small and disappointing class. The tournament lacked spirit and the Summersleave Ball was a bore. Even I, a common servant girl, knew there wasn't a true prince among them.

Time passes and the mist curtain rises. A flock of geese flies by. They form an arrow. I follow their path. They lead me to the mast of another ship and then onward to a third, its boisterous sails billowing in the breeze.

"At least there will be three students this summer. Maybe even a prince for me."

I look to the clouds. "Tell me, Mother. I ask you again. Would it be so wrong to marry a prince for transport?" I laugh and wait, but Mother doesn't answer.

All of the PITs aren't princes, of course. In fact, most are not. They are of royal lineage though, descendents of dukes and earls. The Muffets spend countless hours prettying themselves for the summer boys, working on their perfect gowns for the Summersleave Ball. This is where the princes test out their ballroom dancing skills, and as there are no royal girls here, we Miramore girls get to play princesses for the evening. Even before the rules of the Order changed, the summer visitors always had an interest in us Miramore girls, hoping for a no-hearts-attached summer fling. Now the stakes are raised. Now they may come searching for a girl to make a princess.

Not that the boys of Miramore aren't worthy of our attention. For the most part, they are fine, hardworking young men, but they are bound to service here on the isle. They have neither the freedom nor the means and, as far as I can tell, not the desire either, to leave. They'll never make a girl a princess.

Not that I have ever wanted that. I only wanted Mackree.

There have been some PITs who caught my attention—standing out at first because they were witty or handsome, smart or brave—some even turned my head a bit as they whirled me about at the ball, but then they spoke or acted in a way in which their true character was revealed, and *poof*, the spell was broken.

So many PITs, never a prince.

Another ship approaches now. I turn the rim of my scope. There's a garishly painted mermaid carved on the hull, an audacious yet silent mascot. The mermaid's arms are clasped prisoner-like behind her neck, yet her chest is thrust forward, chin out, face upturned, braving the waves, leading the way.

My stomach grumbles and I reach in my satchel for a still-warm strawberry muffin, tossing some bits to my feathered friends. I brush a crumb from my blouse and wrap my fingers around the oyster shell on the braided seagrass rope. The necklace was a gift for my fifteenth birthday last August.

"Happy birthday, dear daughter," Father had said, placing the simple necklace over my bowed head. He lifted my chin to look at me. "You have your mother's raven hair and her emerald eyes, and her heart open wide as the sea."

"Papa, how you flatter me so." I dusted flecks of flour and cocoa powder from his thick gray beard, remnants of the scrumptious cake he had personally baked for me, much to Nora Baker's annoyance.

"Your mother, Miriam, made this necklace," Father said. "She found this shell as she walked the beach so happily, carrying you nine months heavy inside. It was on that day she chose your name, Gracepearl. 'Our Grace will be a pearl among princes and the world her oyster shall be.'"

Oh, how I miss my mother. She died when I was eight.

My mind's album is filled with vivid scenes—lullabies and nursery rhymes, beach walks, forest talks, picnics and adventures, reading snuggled side by side, dancing by the firelight. Then my memory book ends abruptly, so many pages blank.

It could have ended there, but no. My beautiful and brilliant mother had a wonderful idea. In the months before her death from consumption, unbeknownst to me, she planned ten years' worth of birthday presents, one special surprise a year, which she instructed Papa to give me in the precise order outlined in a letter.

Father keeps Mother's birthday presents stowed in a purple trunk with a brass lock beneath his bed. He wears the key on a thin leather rope around his neck—silly goose of him, really, as I would never peek. I wouldn't want to spoil the surprise!

Each year when Father gives me the next gift, he tells me the story connected with it. The spyglass was a gift to my mother from her father, the jewel-framed mirror from her mother. The eider-bark journal contains my own mother's skillful sketches and descriptions of every flower and tree on Miramore, each animal, fish, and all things with wings. And so, every year on my birthday, my mother's treasures become my treasures.

Soon I will be sixteen. Mother said that "soon" I would choose. How soon is soon? Does she mean on my birthday? If so, choose what? Choose to stay or leave?

The only way I can leave is to marry a prince. Why doesn't that notion inspire me?

When I was little I play-dreamed that I would one day marry Mackree. Then for near a decade we were as sister and brother, best-best friends. But this past year things grew awkward between us. Mackree's feelings for me altered in a way I was not ready for. He hinted of marrying. Me? I know now I want something more than the wifely life on Miramore, cooking and cleaning and such. I want to make a difference out there in the world beyond, serve in some purposeful way. I want to mark my footprints, my *handprints*, on a bigger beach. And besides, I'm a horrible cook.

In school, when we would read the stories of noble heroes throughout time, the Muffets swooned, seeing themselves swept away by charming princes. Me? I wondered how Joan of Arc felt as she charged forward to save her people.

Mackree is right. We're too old for skipping stones. Now that he rebukes me, it is good that I set my sights elsewhere. Maybe this is the summer. Miramore, however lovely, has grown smaller than a water closet. I feel a pull like the powerful tide, but where, where, does it lead me?

More time passes and the sun finally claims its throne in the sky, uncurling long finger rays of gold. "Good. An eighth ship." I scan wide across the horizon and then I see them. One . . . two . . . three . . . four more. *Twelve.*

A banner year indeed! Every branch of the Royal Order has sent a prince for training. "To the docks!" I stuff my spyglass in my satchel and turn.

Caw, caw, the gull screeches. I look back.

The bird hops off the sill and flits toward me, landing at my feet. Its beady black eye meets mine for a second, then it *caws* meaningfully again and flies up to ledge.

What is it? I move to the ledge and look down at the water.

There is another ship.

That cannot be. I count them again, poking my finger in the air, one to three, until I reach thirteen. Indeed, a thirteenth ship approaches Miramore.

How is that possible? There are only twelve branches of the Royal Order. Each branch sends one ship. No merchant vessels or recreational boats ever make their way to Miramore. Safe passage here is a well-guarded secret, only known to the royal families. You will not find the island on a seafaring map, nor divined by navigation device. And if the constant circle of fog around the isle, as thick as Saturn's ring, is not enough to keep visitors away, the dangerous spiked shoals on the left arc, like the spears of armored knights, or the fiery whirlpools that can suck a boat down into a dragon-fierce inferno on the right arc, would discourage an idle explorer.

The only people who come here are the PITs. Their trusted captains deposit them in June and return to collect them in September along with the reams of cotton and wool, linen and lace ordered from the mills. Only these faithful old seamen know the way.

A thirteenth ship? Who can this be? I turn my spyglass for a closer look. Judging from the boat, this royal is not wealthy. He comes in a simple vessel, two modest tarp sails without adornment, no regal coat of arms.

There is the captain at the wheel, but where is his royal passenger? This ship bears no such grandeur as a lower deck. It is really no more than a fishing boat.

Hmmm, how interesting. How exciting!

I gather my skirts about me and hurry down the tower steps to find Lu and Nuff.

What are little boys made of?
Snips and snails,
And puppy dogs' tails!
That's what little boys are made of.

What are little girls made of?
Sugar and spice,
And everything nice!
That's what little girls are made of.

CHAPTER 3

The PITs

Rushing down the hill toward the beach to meet my friends, I pause to pluck a callaberry blossom and loop the stem around my ear. The red flower with a yellow heart is lovelier than the ruby hair brooch that brash PIT from Sycamore, Aldous, offered me last summer. His girlfriend, a duke's daughter, insisted he take the ornament for the summer to remember her by. Sir Aldous had the nerve to say I could "borrow it" in exchange for a kiss. "Pig's chance of that," I told him.

Hopefully Nuff is finished ironing the royals' fine

linen sheets and Lu is done dusting their quarters. Thanks to Father, on this arrival day, I am not due in the kitchen until later.

"Have fun, Gracepearl," Father said this morning in the kitchen, feathers flying up about his happy face as he plucked the freshly slaughtered chickens for tomorrow's feast.

"And give those poor princes a pity-try this year," Nora Baker shouted to me as she took a tray of muffins from the oven. "If yer lucky maybe one'll call ya princess."

I smiled and caught a feather in the air. "Or I could stick this feather in a prince's hat and call *him* macaroni." Swiping two hot muffins I dashed off, Father's laughter ringing sweet in my ears.

Down one flight of stone steps, then another, I reach the beach, toss off my sandals, and sink my feet in the cool soft sand.

"Gracepearl! Gracepearl!" Lu and Nuff call from an elevated spot by the docks.

Over there are the Muffets in their matching pink shawls primping their hair and fidgeting about for the best spots for the princes to see them.

Maneuvering through the crowd, I search faces for Mackree as I go.

As they have on this first day of summer for ages, the people of Miramore have gathered here to welcome the royal boys. Fishermen, farmers, carpenters, weavers, tinkers, butlers and scullery maids, stable hands, grounds-keepers, those who toil in the orchards and vineyards and vegetable gardens, the flax and wheat and cotton fields, the farms and the fabric mills. Miramore exists primarily as a summer school where royals learn the charming arts. Secondarily we provide reams of wool and cotton fabrics, linens and fine embroidered pieces for the wealthy families of the Order.

The isle provides us food aplenty and surely everything a cook could wish for. Father furnishes delicious meals for the professors who remain here all year long, but as he would be the first to boast, the food he prepares in the summer is truly fit for a king.

Over there on the raised dais are Headmistress Jule and the instructors in their university robes. I scrunch my nose as I do at the smell of blue cheese at the sight of mean pockmark-faced Pillage, Professor Emeritus in the military arts. He once taught for the House of Ash and has come to Miramore for the warm climate and fresh air to soothe his smoke-diseased lungs. It's rumored that Pillage wants to teach this year, but we can't imagine he would stoop to teach the charming arts. Not that he has an ounce of knowledge on such matters—he is the least charming man I've ever met.

Reaching my friends, I hug them. "Lu! Nuff!"

"Gracie," Lu says, relieved, "thank goodness. Where have you been?"

"We feared you'd miss the rating," Nuff says.

"Wouldn't miss it for the world," I say. Inside I'm thinking, *Especially this year.* But even as I think this I wonder how I could leave Father and Mackree and my dear best friends, Lu and Nuff.

Sweet Lu, short and plump, pale and pretty, a heart as good as gold. She wants a big family, a gaggle of children. Nuff and I tease her about turning into that lady who lived in a shoe who had so many children she didn't know what to do.

And Nuff, beautiful Nuff, tall, thin, and ebony-skinned, smart and so quick-witted, the sweet aroma of frangipani always about her. Nuff adores Miramore and insists she could never leave. Nuff's mother, so wise in formulating soaps for their laundry work, is equally gifted at crafting luscious perfumes from the sweet petals of the island's flowers. She is teaching her daughter her trade. One day Nuff will take her mother's place. Any prince who falls in love with Nuff will have to fall for this island too.

The trumpet blows. The first ship lands. A roar of excited chatter rises up.

"This prince is from Oakland," Nuff says, pointing to the large brown-leafed coat of arms on the sail.

Of all the forest trees, I like the oak least of all. Its fat leaves make heavy wet piles on the ground over winter, blocking sunlight from the flowers in spring.

Two docksmen work to secure the ropes. The Oakland captain lowers the wooden steps. The crowd hushes. A red feather is the first to appear, then a brown velvet hat, yellow curls, and long bony nose on a powder white face as this round-bellied royal one ascends from his cabin.

"He looks our age," Lu says.

Standing on the deck this first PIT sniffs the air and squints his eyes as if he is not accustomed to sun. His captain supports the PIT's elbow as he waddles down the steps to the dock. This PIT could use some exercise. I start to say as much, then stop. Lu forever battles with her weight and I'd never want to hurt her feelings again. Last year I kindly suggested she might want to eat more apples than apple tarts, and I offended her greatly.

The wind whips off the Oakland PIT's velvet hat and drops it into the sea, where it skits across the surface like one of Mackree's skipping stones. The stones I used to collect for him on my morning beach walks.

Without a word of instruction, Lu's little brother, Leem, and his friend Brine tear off their shirts, run to the water, and dive toward the floating hat. Reaching it first, Leem holds up his dripping trophy, waving it triumphantly in the air. He swims back to shore, hoists himself up on the dock, and wrings the water from the hat as he has no doubt watched his mum do with towels countless times. Then with a clumsy but practiced bow, Leem kneels and presents the hat to the royal.

"Your Highness," Leem shouts in a too-loud voice, and then steps back reverently.

The royal one of Oakland, oval shaped like a fat farm egg, scowls as if he's been proffered a rat. "Toss it there, boy," he says, pointing to a refuse barrel.

Some Muffets giggle as if this is amusing.

"He's not very nice," Lu says.

Leem does as he is instructed, then walks quickly off the dock, head down, arms crossed tightly over his shivering chest. Anger rises within me. Poor Leem.

The Oakland captain hands a missive to the Welcome Guard and after a prolonged blowing by the trumpeter, the guard announces: "Presenting His Royalness Sir Humbert of Oakland."

I note Leem's face, still flushed red with shame, then turn my gaze back to the PIT fussing with his preposterous blond curls. *You're no prince, Sir Humbert.*

"Well, girls?" Nuff says with a sniff, pen poised. "How do you rate him?"

We give stars, one to five, one being the lowest, five the top.

"One," Lu says.

"Zero," I say. "He's Humpty Dumpty with hair."

◇◇◇◇◇

The second ship to dock bears the insignia of the House of Ashland. This PIT politely refuses his captain's offer of assistance, stepping out of his cabin, down the stairs to the dock, where he stops to survey the shore before him.

"Ooh, *handsome*," Lu says. "And older than us. Nineteen, twenty maybe?"

"Why hasn't he been here before?" Nuff says.

The festooned display of badges and medals on this PIT's fine fitted jacket glints in the sun. "Most likely he's been at war," I say.

"Presenting Sir Richard of Ashland," the guard calls out. The Muffets *ooh* and *aah* and jostle to be noticed. There's movement from the dais as Professor Pillage stands with a flourish and salutes. The Miramore men copy him.

Sir Richard has neatly shaven brown hair and stunning blue eyes, cheeks and jaw chiseled sharp. We curtsy as he passes. His eyes meet mine and he smiles. This soldier prince has potential. I'm about to say as much when I see Lu's face, eyes glossy wide and cheeks flushed crimson as her curls.

"Five stars," Lu whispers, "fifteen . . . fifty. I am smitten to the core." She clutches her palm to her chest with great drama.

"Steady, girl," Nuff says. "We don't know what he's made of yet."

"Oh, Nuff," Lu sighs. "A handsome soldier of royal birth, what more do you need to know?"

Nuff looks at me and rolls her eyes. I shake my head and smile.

Next to arrive is Sir Peter of Elmland, long black hair in a ponytail, a silver loop hanging from his ear. The Muffets titter and wave. As Sir Peter passes, his piercing dark eyes meet mine and I feel a flutter inside. Another possibility, this pirate prince.

"That one's a looker," Nuff says, smiling as she makes notes.

"He's most likely a rogue," Lu says. "Remember that long-locks one Ivan, here last summer, got me in a hornet's nest of trouble?"

Sir Ivan cornered Lu for a kiss and when she refused he accused her of being a thief. Lu's worm-spined father unfairly punished her. Heaven forbid a PIT ever tried to hurt me. Father would chop off his head with a carving knife and toss him to the swine.

"We shouldn't hold a ponytail against him," Nuff says, still following Sir Peter with her eyes. "I'd give him five stars. What say you, Grace?"

Five stars is our highest rating. "Five for his looks anyway," I say.

The sun strengthens. Sweat beads on my brow.

The next arrival is "Sir Henry of Hickory." Sir Henry is short and rotund with closely set eyes, an upturned nose, and ears too large for his head. He hurries past us, head shaking with a nervous twitter.

"He looks like a mouse," Nuff says. "Hickory, dickory . . ." Lu and I join in.

"Hickory, dickory, dock,
The mouse ran up the clock
The clock struck one,
And down he run,
Hickory, dickory, dock."
We end in a gale of laughter.

"We shouldn't be so harsh," I say.

"He didn't hear us," Lu says.

"I'm not so sure," Nuff says. "Those are some serious ears."

❖❖❖❖❖

The morning wears on, eight more ships dock. Eight more captains present letters. Eight more trumpetings. Eight more royals announced. We make notes on each prince in training. I'll have the chance to gather more impressions working the banquet tomorrow night.

The PIT from Maple is muscular and strong. "I'd give him three stars," Nuff says.

Sir Blake of Birch looks studious but weak. "Two," Lu says.

"Three," Nuff counters. "I'd take brains over brawn any day."

"But he looks like one gusty gale could send him flying home," I say, then feel a twinge of guilt. *I know, Mother, it's wrong of me,* casting judgments on first impressions, but what's that they say about love at first sight? I think maybe you know from the start. *Mackree.*

Where is Mackree? I step up on my toes, look all about, but he is not here.

There's a swill of loud chattering as the thirteenth boat makes its final approach. Everyone is excited to see who this arrival will be, for surely he cannot be a prince, all twelve branches being accounted for.

The boat washes in against the dock. The captain, an old man, at least Nora Baker's age, with a sea-roughened face, wild gray hair and beard, is wearing an unusual green leather cape. He waves off the Welcome Guard.

"Just me, Cap'n Jessie . . . Jessie Tru," he says. "No royals aboard. I'm here on business of the Order is all."

Lu, Nuff, and I exchange looks. How very curious. We watch as Captain Jessie slings a canvas bag on his back and heads up the hill, his left leg limping a bit.

Mary, Mary quite contrary,
How does your garden grow?
With silver bells, and cockleshells,
And pretty maids all in a row.

CHAPTER 4

The Rhymes

"As I was going along, long, long, singing a comical song, song, song, the lane that I took was so long, long, long, and so I went singing along." I sing as I head to the gardens the next morning to gather the vegetables Father needs for the banquet.

Mother taught me all the rhymes. First how to sing them, then how to read them. The one we loved best was Old King Cole. The name was like our name, Coal, for the black lumps that fuel our fires. Father played his fiddle with joyous glee as Mother and I danced happily, *whee!!!*

When Lu and Nuff came for tea parties, Mother taught them the rhymes as well. The little ditties became like our own special language. When Sally Tailor, the seamstress's daughter, and her friends started acting silly around boys, making believe they were scared of spiders and such to get the boys' attention, we named them the Muffets like Little Miss Muffet. Those girls seem to care for nothing except primping their hair and fussing with clothes, spinning webs to snare a husband, preferably a prince.

Maybe someday I will pass on Mother's frayed-edged book of rhymes to my own child—teaching the words and the melodies, turning the pages my mother's hands turned, touching the very words she touched. I always assumed that one day, far in the future, Mackree would be my husband and we would have children, a girl and a boy. But now . . .

As I pass the carrot patch, two sets of furry ears perk up. "No worries, little friends," I call to them. "No carrots on Cook's menu today."

First to the tomatoes. How pretty they are, rows and rows of tall, thick, prickly vines straining with fat garnet jewels. The sun heats my back as I bend to pluck the first of thirty as Father instructed. In celebration of the PITs' arrival, tonight's Welcome Banquet will be especially fine. Father is thrilled that he'll be cooking for such a large class this year. "The more the merrier," he always says.

Those royal boys may be used to the finest food in all the world, Humpty Dumpty Sir Humbert especially, as evidenced by his shape, but none has ever experienced

Cook's masterful work, the deliciously inventive pairings and artfully presented plates that he will create tonight.

My mouth waters in anticipation. For on each banquet night, once the princes have retired to the den for cribbage or chess, Father serves a second, I think even finer, meal for all the attending servants.

I lift a tomato from its fuzzy green stem, brush the smooth warm skin against my face, breathing in deeply of its earthy scent. *Ahhh.*

Counting out thirty, exactly thirty, no need to be wasteful, as Father says, I set the basket of tomatoes in the shade and wipe the sweat from my forehead. Taking the spade from its casing tied to a loop on the belt of my skirt, I swing the other basket and move to another section of the hill, where I kneel to dig potatoes.

Potatoes are harder work. I double the lower folds of my skirt to make a padding for my knees. The sun beats without a break on my back. I stop and shed my outer sweater, tying it about my waist. I turn my face toward the sea, welcoming a bit of breeze, then dig my spade back in the dirt to unearth another thick brown tuber.

"Well, what have we here?" A boy's voice breaks the silence.

Humpty Dumpty. He is wearing a wide-brimmed hat, no doubt to protect his thin shell from the sun. He holds a book and a butterfly net. Raising the binoculars that dangle from his neck, he stares at me as if I'm some strange bird he hopes to identify. He stares and stares and stares.

"Sir, how dare you study me so!" I stand up, spade in hand, tossing a potato into the basket.

Sir Humpty cackles like a barnyard hen. "My apologies, fair maiden." He fingers a yellow curl and sniffs the air. "I'm simply getting the lay of the land, examining the flora and fauna of the isle. I find the present sight most . . . *appealing* indeed." His thin lips rise on one side into a most unattractive smirk.

"Well I'm no flower or fawn, sir. You would do well to cast your gaze elsewhere." I'm reminded of that rank Sir Ivan last year, how he felt he could take advantage of Lu because she was a servant.

The royal boy's smirk ceases and his nose stiffens. "I will gaze at whatever I desire," he says in the same rapid cold cadence he used with poor Leem at the docks yesterday morning. His eyes move down and up again, taking in the full view of me.

I move fast toward him until the tip of my dirt-covered spade nearly grazes his fat dimpled chin. "Then I suggest you never desire me, sir."

"Gracepearl!" The sound of Nuff's call pierces the air. "Gracepearl! Where are you?" Nuff's voice grows closer, rising up from the berry patches. "Come! Quickly!"

I run toward Nuff, thinking briefly that I should

take the baskets along, Father will be needing them, but they are heavy and would weigh me down. I'll return for them in a moment when hopefully the egg boy will be gone.

There are streams of tears running down Nuff's cheeks, her brown eyes brimming with some sad story like cups of tea waiting to be poured.

"Oh, Gracepearl, I'm sorry," Nuff sobs, clutching me tightly to her chest.

I pull away so I can see her face. "What, Nuff, *what*?"

Nuff's mouth contorts. She sobs and gulps and sobs again. "It's your father. Good Cook. It's his heart."

It's raining, it's pouring.
The old man is snoring.
He went to bed
Where he bumped his head,
And he didn't get up till morning.

CHAPTER 5

The Hospital

Thorns scratch and sting my legs as I race through the raspberry bushes. Later I'll tend to the cuts, this moment all that matters is Father. My heart throbbing, mind screaming, I run. Hold on, Father, I'm coming.

Reaching the dining hall, I storm into the kitchen. Father's workers look toward me with mournful glances.

"They've taken him to hospital," Nora Baker shouts, her fat freckled arms sunk deep in dough. "Wher've ya been, ya goosey girl? Go!"

Nora's words cut me even though I know she doesn't mean to be cruel. Father always says it's just Nora's hard way, like bread left too long in the oven.

I tear across the field and up the road to the hospital, a dreary grim building I've not been to since I pulled the top off a double-decker pot and boiling steam burned my neck. A good salve took the pain away, but not the memory. I am no fan of cooking pots.

Heart pounding, body sweating, I reach the entrance and push open the heavy wooden door, nearly knocking down Captain Jessie Tru, on the other side.

"Oh, sorry, sir," I say, catching my breath.

"Grace," he says, bowing forward in a sweetly chivalrous manner. Rising up he looks in my eyes, his face soft with emotion as if he knows me, and yet we've never met. How does he know my name?

No time for small talk. "Are you okay, sir? Here, sit for a moment." I motion him toward a bench.

"Yer like a gale force, you are," he says with a laugh that deepens the wrinkles on his wind-battered face. He coughs a deep garrulous cough.

"Are you sick, Captain Jessie?" I say. "You've only just arrived and . . ."

"Bit of a toe fungus is all," he says, raising his left boot. "Nature of the job. Some days ya just can't get dry at sea."

I nod as if I understand and then, assured he's all right, I set off to find my father.

There is no one at the front desk. I start down the hall, ducking my head in first one, then another, then a third room. "Father!" I race to his bedside.

His eyes are closed but his thick chest moves up and down as he snores.

"Thank heavens." I wrap my arms about him and let the sobs come.

A nurse comes into the room. *"Shhhh,"* she admonishes, finger stamping her tight pinched lips. She motions for me to join her in the hallway.

There is a wool blanket at the base of Father's bed. I pull it up over him to keep him warm. "Be right back," I whisper, kissing his cheek.

Out in the hall I say, "I'm Cook's daughter, Grace-pearl."

"Yes," says the nurse coldly.

"What happened?" I ask.

"A heart attack," she says, sallow-faced and bird thin as if she hasn't had a good meal in years.

"How can that be? He was fine this morning."

"I am not the doctor, miss. You may speak with Dr. Jeffers when he makes his evening rounds, but I would say it has something to do with your father's . . . fondness for food." She shakes her head disapprovingly. "He's got more blubber than the whales that used to fuel every lamp on Mira—"

"How dare you speak of my father like that!" My face flushes hot. "What is your name? I'll have you reported . . ."

"Nurse Hartling," she says with a sniff, adjusting her starched white cap. "And my apologies, miss, but you would do well to put your father on a diet."

I resist the urge to slap this brazen bird. I take a breath and let it out slowly, the temper-taming trick Father taught me. "Will he be all right, Nurse?"

"That's for Doctor to judge," Nurse Hartling says, checking her watch, "but he's been resting with ease for some two to three hours now, with no further round of pain, and that is generally a good sign."

Dear Father has been lying in this hospital bed for three hours while I was sparring with fool Humpty in the garden? My throat clenches. I gulp back tears. "May I stay with him?"

"It's best you let him sleep," the pinch-nosed nurse says. "He should not move or try to speak or be troubled by any . . . emotional outbursts from visitors. The longer he rests, the better he will be."

"Very well, then. I thank you, Nurse Hartling, for the fine care I know you will bestow upon my father." That's another good lesson I learned from Father, a bit of honey can sweeten the bitterest tea.

I pause at the doorway. I touch my fingers to my lips and blow a kiss to my father, speaking silent words of love I am certain he can hear.

The man in the wilderness asked of me
How many strawberries grew in the sea
I answered him as I thought good
As many as red herrings grow in the wood.

CHAPTER 6

Mackree, My Heart

Although duty calls me to retrieve the baskets from the gardens and take my post in the kitchen, my heart leads me elsewhere.

I walk briskly past the stone-cold chapel with its ornately carved doors, incense, and stained-glass windows—that place never held much joy for me—then up the hill to the forest and a certain well-worn path.

Into the woods I step. It is cool and quiet here. Closing my eyes, I take a long deep breath of my favorite scent, that comforting nurturing spicy aroma. *Pine.*

Hmmmm. A memory. It was late November, I was six or seven. Mother and I had filled a burlap sack full of pine needles. Back at the cottage, first checking that Father was still away, Mother helped me cut two rectangles from a piece of red velvet cloth. She turned the pieces so that the lining faced outward and then she showed me how to make a row of stitches an inch in from the edge, down one of the long sides of the rectangle, across one of the short ends, then up the other long side. I was sewing!

We turned the material inside out again and then filled the hollow space with pine needles, stuff-stuff-stuffing them down into the corners until I had a plump pillow in my hands. Next, Mother showed me a more difficult, prettier stitch for closing up the opening, then helped me sew "Merry Christmas" in thick green thread against the red.

Oh, how delighted Father was that holiday morning, so proud of my artistry. "The best gifts are the ones you make," he said.

And all these years later, even though it is a seasonal item that might just as well be tossed into the holiday box with the candles, bells, and decorations, that little red pillow rests atop Father's own sleeping pillow and it still smells of pine—the ever-growing, ever-green tree. I think of the branches of the Royal Order. Why is there no House of Pine? I must ask Father about that.

Deeper into the forest I walk, the path less trodden now. I stop by an oak tree and stoop to pick up an acorn, smiling at the tiny brown face with the pointed cap. Another memory comes. Mother and I had finished a forest picnic and I began collecting acorns in our empty basket. Mother found two sharp-edged stones and we etched eyes, a nose, and a smile onto each acorn's face. We gathered wildflowers on our way home. Later, we crushed goldenrod to make yellow, cornflowers for blue, poppies for red, and then we painted the acorn people's caps. I set them on the windowsill to dry.

Father roared with laughter when he saw them. "What a nutty little family," he said. After dinner, Father took out his fiddle and he played a jig, and Mother and I danced. After a bit, Father set the fiddle down and joined us circling about the room, so happy, the three of us. Whee!

Now Mother is gone. Please, not Father too. *Please, God, don't let Father die. Oh, Mother, how I wish you were here.*

◇◇◇◇◇

I pass the kettle pond where Mackree and I first held hands. Mackree, my heart. My chest clenches at the thought of him. I walk between two birch trees, by the brambleberries, part the thicket of heavy branches that swing back like doors behind me, and now, at last, I am here. My secret sanctuary. My place of peace. And though I have no memory of having ever been here with my mother, I feel her in the soft pale-green moss, in the grace of the filigreed fern, in the giggling of the leaves, in the sunlight dappling down through spaces in the pine green canopy to gently warm my face.

"Mother," I cry as I drop to my knees. "Please say Father will live. Please, Mother, talk to me."

Only silence.

I wipe my face on my skirt, blow my nose on my sleeve. I lie back on the soft moss carpet and stare up at the leafy dome. Worried thoughts and garbled notions muddle my mind. I try to send them off like waves from the shore so I can hear Mother's reply. I am certain she will answer me.

I close my eyes.

Soon I see the faces. People, young and old. Their troubled eyes search mine "What can I do?" I ask. Now I see myself standing on the beach. I am stepping onto a boat. A voice calls out. It sounds like "Pearl." But the wind is strong. I cannot tell who it is. The boat rocks. I sit quickly so I won't fall. A wave slaps high and sprays my face . . .

"Pearl." The voice calls out to me again.

A boy's voice. I know that voice. Someone shakes my arm. I open my eyes.

"Mackree!" His name escapes with a squeal of glee. How wonderful. Can this be true or is this still the dream?

"Pearl," he says. "Are you okay?" His rich brown hair hangs so long now it nearly covers his eyes. I brush away the bangs so I can peer into those deep dark violet pools. My heart fills to near bursting with joy. Mackree, pronounced "muh-*kree*." Mother said that in an old language *mo chroi* meant *my heart*. Mackree, my heart, indeed.

Mackree flinches as though my touch burns his forehead. He shakes his hair till it covers his eyes again. He turns from me.

"Just checkin' you were all right," he says. "I heard about Cook."

"Thank you," I say. "I'm so glad you came. But how did you find me?" I sit up. "I didn't know anyone knew of this place."

Mackree looks quickly at me and then away. "I know all about you, Pearl."

I smile. *Pearl*. Mackree's the only one who calls me just Pearl. I stand and brush the moss and pine needles from my skirt. Joy rises within me. "I'm so glad you're here. How are you? What have you been up to these—"

"If you're okay," he says curtly, "I'm off."

"No, Mackree. Wait. Stay awhile, please?"

He walks away.

"Stop, please! I know you still care for me."

"And that is why I must go," he says in barely a whisper.

"Mackree, why?" A sob escapes.

He reels around angrily. "Your heart calls you from Miramore, Pearl. You have said it yourself many times of late. All your strange dreams . . . things I can't fathom.

I wonder too about the world beyond the water, but I cannot leave. No princesses coming to Miramore who might be taken with me."

I laugh. "Oh, you are wrong," I say. "You are the handsomest boy on the island."

"I have a duty to my family, Pearl, and to the Order."

"But what of *me*?" I say.

Our eyes lock. My heart pounds

"I would do anything for you, Pearl. I would give you the world. But the world you want is not mine to give. Only a prince can take you there."

"But—"

"We're done, Pearl. Leave me be. Find a prince this summer and go quickly. I grow my hair long so I won't see."

Mackree parts the pine branches and is gone.

"Wait, Mackree, wait!" I shout, running after him.

But Mackree was always faster than me. When I reach the clearing, he is gone.

I look up at the sky. The sun hangs low. It must be near dinnertime. Oh no, the vegetables. In Father's absence, Nora will command the kitchen. Even though she knows Cook's in the hospital, she'll still be expecting the vegetables.

I race up the hill to the garden. Out of breath, panting, I reach the place where I left the baskets. The potatoes are there, but what of the tomatoes? I look up and down the vegetable rows. Finally I spot the basket, there at the far edge of the garden, where the land drops off quickly into cliffs.

I reach the basket. It's empty. I look down over the cliff.

There are the tomatoes, splattered bloody red over the pale sea-burnished rocks. Gulls are swooping down, picking at the feast, trying to beat the tide, which will wash it all away.

Sir Humbert, it had to have been. "What an evil creature you are," I shout.

Humpty Dumpty sat on a wall,
Humpty Dumpty had a great fall.

The rhyme taunts loudly in my brain as I race to the kitchen with the potatoes.

All the king's horses
And all the king's men
Couldn't put Humpty together again.

Or the tomatoes, for that matter.

Sing a song of sixpence,
A pocket full of rye,
Four and twenty blackbirds,
Baked in a pie;
When the pie was opened,
The birds began to sing;
Wasn't that a dainty dish
To set before a king?

CHAPTER 7

The Welcome Banquet

After bearing Nora's tongue-lashing for being late and tomato-less, I set to peeling a mound of potatoes. When I go to get my cloak at the end of the day, I see one of the other kitchen workers, "Tattlebug" as I call her, as she is forever listening in to conversations and spreading gossip like a flea among dung heaps. She's standing at the hallway window looking out, giggling. She has my spyglass! Just then Nora calls me urgently and I go to answer her. When I return, Tattlebug is gone, my spyglass back in the pocket of my cloak. So Nell Tinker's a gossip and now a snitch too.

After work I hurry home to dress for the banquet. I wash up and put on the emerald green dress Father says matches my eyes. I slip the oyster shell necklace around my neck and weave a green satin ribbon through my hair.

There. I smile at myself in my mother's gem-rounded looking glass. Tonight I will be wearing an apron, a kitchen servant, yes, but I may also woo a prince. Surely Father's service bondage could be lifted now that he is ill. If I become a princess, I will see that he enjoys a life of comfort. He'll never have to cook again, and neither will I, for that matter. Oatmeal is my best dish, but practice, practice as I've tried, it still comes out all sticky clumps, despite the extra sugar lumps.

Pease porridge hot, pease porridge cold,
Pease porridge in the pot, nine days old . . .
That rhyme always makes me smile.
Spell me that in four letters.
I will: T-H-A-T

❖❖❖❖❖

Before I leave, I step into Father's empty room. There, on the table by his bed, is the giant purple-rimmed clamshell I gave him as a birthday gift one year when I was little. "A bowl for the ashes from your pipe," I suggested. He hugged me as if I'd given him a crate full of gold. And now, even though Father stopped smoking right after Mother died and never took it up again, just like the pine pillow, Father keeps this gift still. Now the clamshell is a candy dish, always filled with something sweet.

Passing the wooden bookcase by the hearth, I notice one spine jutting out from the rest. It's the book of history Mother schooled me with. When we read about kings and queens who waged war against one another for power or land, knights with crosses emblazoned on their shields, fighting in the "name of God," I would get angry and ask Mother how that could be true. I didn't think God cared about who owned what. Surely God cared more about the peasants lining the roadways, hands outstretched, begging for pity coins or crusts of bread, bowing and curtsying respectfully as royal coaches rumbled by. "That's right, darling," Mother would say to me. "You are learning well."

I flip through the old book, noting the ripped-out pages, always a curiosity to me. Here's the section where the branches of the Royal Order are called . . . Oak, Ash, Elm, and so forth . . . the page ripped after the name of the twelfth, then onward random words etched out, leaving holes like rats had nibbled for dinner, more pages gone here and there, and then the last chapter torn out completely. When I would ask Mother about the missing pieces she would wave it off lightly. "It's of no concern to you, dear daughter. Some history is better off forgotten."

As I walk to the royal dining hall, I think about the PITs. How dashing Sir Richard, the soldier prince, smiled at me on the beach. And ponytailed Sir Peter, the pirate prince, how his dark eyes locked with mine. Both beautiful outside, but what of within? Will their inside colors be five-star too? Honesty, integrity, compassion . . .

Mother said I will have a "choice." Possibly a choice between two princes? I giggle. Gracepearl, you gallop ahead of yourself.

⋄⋄⋄⋄⋄

Outside the royal hall the heady aroma of food sweeps over me like a sea squall, and as I enter the kitchen the most delicious wave nearly topples me down. I think to save a plate to bring to Father later, but I have a notion that the goat-cheese-stuffed baked chicken, potato soufflé, brandied mushrooms, and such will not be on Cook's hospital diet tonight. I think of pencil-nosed Nurse Hartling and hope she's treating Father kindly.

"Here ya go, girl," Nora barks when she sees me, thrusting a too-big gray apron in my hands and motioning to a silver serving dish with two wells full of salad dressing. "Blueberry or champagne vinaigrette," she says. "Take a ladle for each."

"Ooh, fancy," I say as a compliment, but Nora ignores it, never one for praise.

I enter the dining room and look toward the two long

46

tables where the PITs are seated. Sir Humpty's eyes catch mine and I swear he is laughing at me. I scowl and move toward my post, circulating around the professors' table, offering dressings for the fresh green but tomato-less salad. Nora cleverly thought to substitute strawberries. What a good idea. She's surprising me. I bet they taste lovely.

Headmistress Jule is seated at the head table, orchestrating conversation with her signature ease and grace. Slight as a fairy, she sits propped on pillows to compensate for her height, her white hair swept up and clasped with jeweled pins, a shimmery silver dress fanning out around her. I note the tiny velvet pouch by her wine goblet. She keeps her honey sweetdrops in there. Lady Jule is known for her sugary tooth.

"Blueberry or champagne vinaigrette, Lady Jule?"

"Champagne, thank you, Gracepearl." She touches my arm as I ladle out the dressing. "How pray tell is dear Cook?"

Lady Jule favors Father as much as her sweets. "Better, ma'am. Thank you."

"Here," she says, proffering me the velvet pouch. "Bring these to Cook with my best wishes for a swift and full recovery."

"I will, Lady Jule, thank you." I slip the pouch into my apron pocket and continue down the line.

I hear giggling and note four small dirty boots

sticking out from beneath the draperies, holes in two of the soles. Leem and Brine have snuck in again this year, I see, hoping to sample the succulent fare. Nora Baker will bat their bums home with a broom if she discovers they are there. Leem peeks out. I smile and wink, tapping my finger to my lips, reminding him to be quiet.

When I approach Professor Pillage he is crinkling his nose at the salad, stabbing out the strawberries as if they are beetles. He waves away my offer of dressing, without so much as a "no thank you." Professor Millington, instructor of Manners, Protocol, and Etiquette, *tsk, tsks* at him. "Not a very good example for the princes," she says.

Lady Jule taps her crystal water goblet with a spoon and rises. The room soon comes to attention. "Royal visitors, distinguished faculty, loyal staff. As headmistress of the Miramore Academy of the Charming Arts, it is my great pleasure to welcome . . ."

Nora and I stand along the wall at attention, listening to the speech with the other kitchen servants. Tattlebug is hovering by us. She has long had a crush on Mackree and likes to report to him on any snippets of our conversation she can overhear.

Nora is wearing the tall white hat of the lead chef, an honor I'm certain Father would have insisted upon, and yet it makes me sad to see. I tell Nora about Captain

Jessie arriving as he did on a thirteenth ship saying he was here on the "king's business."

"*Ahh. . . .*" Nora sucks in air. "Jessie Tru?" She turns away. "Already?" she whispers to herself, but I hear.

I begin to question her, but then the gong chimes and we must be silent.

Headmistress Jule announces each PIT by name and each young man stands to be recognized. The professors clap. We servants bow or curtsy. Pillage applauds a particularly loud and long time for Sir Richard, who seems uncomfortable being singled out from the others.

Humility, I think to myself. A lovely quality, Sir Richard.

Almost as if Sir Richard heard my thoughts, his eyes glance about the room. When they meet mine, he smiles.

The smile is not lost on Nora, who nudges me with her elbow, nor on the nosey Tattlebug. "Oooh," she says, "looks like Mackree has competition."

When Sir Humpty is introduced, I can feel him staring at me, but I refuse to look his way. I think of toying with his dessert plate. Maybe I'll tuck a bonus into his berry shortcake, a bee or a . . . *No*, that wouldn't do. If discovered, Nora might be blamed.

Lady Jule introduces the faculty.

"Professor Millington . . . Manners, Protocol, and Etiquette . . .

"Professor Quill . . . Letters . . ."

I can almost see Professor Quill pulling the ever-present feather quill pen from behind his ear, scrolling it through the air as he explains his area of expertise to the PITs on the opening day of class, "words, words, beautiful words . . . love letters, poetry, sonnets and rhymes, etcetera, etcetera . . ."

"Madame Bella . . . Ballroom dancing."

"Bella, bella," Professor Quill says, and Madame Bella smiles approvingly.

"Madame Bella will see that our royal charges are well-heeled in the waltz before the Summersleave Ball," Lady Jule continues.

"Professor Gossimer . . . Language and Conversation . . .

"Professor Daterly . . . Special Occasions . . .

"Professor Blunderfuss . . . the Sports of Kings. Professor Blunderfuss will be overseeing the ever-popular tournament, which we look forward to in the coming weeks."

I think of Mackree, who works in the stables. Tonight Mackree is mucking out horse dung, no doubt, pitch-forking heaps of hay, filling the troughs with water. He is a fine rider, the best on Miramore, fast and controlled. Mackree could race any prince and win. I have watched him these many summers as he watched the royal visitors mount the horses he raised and trained, his face a potent double potion of envy and shame.

Professor Millington discreetly passes Lady Jule a note.

Lady Jule reads it, raises her chin, and sniffs the air. It must be some matter of royal protocol, which Professor Millington has just ruled upon.

Lady Jule shrugs her lovely shoulders ever so slightly, almost indiscernibly, as if to say *All right then, if I absolutely must.* "And finally, it is my pleasure to introduce Professor Edwin Pillage, Distinguished Professor Emeritus of the Military Arts, Ashland Academy, visiting with us this summer on Miramore."

Professor Gossimer raises her hand to be recognized. "And what will Professor Pillage be teaching?" She sounds distressed, as if she is unhappy about this news.

"We are still discussing that," Lady Jule says sharply.

"Oooh, a battle's brewing," Tattlebug says with a sneeze. That girl is forever sneezing and wiping her nose. Thank goodness her job is washing dishes and not preparing the food. She comes so close to my face I can smell her nasty oniony breath.

"Lady Jule doesn't want Pillage here. She's no fan of his field of study," Tattlebug says, boastful with her gossip. "I heard her say 'Miramore's mission is charms, not arms.'"

It's no secret Professor Pillage thinks the summer classes here are foolish. He wants Lady Jule to let him offer "real man" courses, hunting and cock-fighting and such. And this year, he insists a race be added to Tournament Day. In the past, the tournament has been mostly for show, the newly charming princes trotting about for our applause. This year, thanks to Pillage, they will compete for the Order's accolades and a large gleaming trophy.

After the berry shortcakes and chocolate truffles are served and the princes begin retiring to the den, I load a silver tray with dishes quickly, hoping to make it to the hospital before Father retires for the night. I stack the plates as high as I dare and turn just as Leem is sneaking out from his under-the-table picnic with Brine. I trip. The fine china dishes crash to the floor, with a sound surely heard around the island.

Sir Richard rises from his nearby seat. He smiles as he notes Leem dashing back under the tablecloth.

"What's this, what's this," Nora Baker shouts, bustling out from the kitchen, her face damp with sweat. Tattlebug is right behind her.

"I'm sorry," I say, "clumsy me." Little Leem has had enough shame. I won't let him bear Nora's wrath too.

"What's the matter with you, girl?" Nora says, her face reddening.

"Gracepearl broke the best dishes," Tattlebug tattles.

Nora is so mad she could spit. She looks to Sir Richard. "I'm sorry, Your Highness."

"No, madame chef, it is I who must apologize," Sir Richard says. "I startled the lady." He bends to retrieve a dish. I do the same. Our eyes meet and he smiles with an ever so slight tilt of his head, showing me he knows about the two food pirates in hiding. How sweet of him to protect Leem and me. This prince needs no class in charm.

"Gracepearl will pick up that mess, Prince," Nora says, huffing disapprovingly.

"Gracepearl," Sir Richard says softly, "what a lovely name." He stands and offers me his hand. He helps me up. His hand is strong. My heart skips a bit.

Sir Richard turns toward Nora. "I was actually coming to the kitchen to seek you out, madame chef. I wanted to compliment you on a truly scrumptious banquet." He taps his stomach. Nora smiles despite herself.

"Would you see fit to fix a snack for me for later?" Sir Richard asks her.

"Of course," Nora says, face gleaming. "Come along, Gracepearl," she says to me. "You go along, sir, and enjoy the games with the other princes. I'll have Grace bring you a basket right away."

I finish picking up the broken china. In the kitchen, Nora slices chicken and slathers slices of fresh herb bread with gingered mayonnaise, humming a happy tune. She takes some pickles from the barrel. Fills a paper bag with sweet-potato chips. Wraps two raspberry tarts.

Puts it all in a wicker basket with a checkered cloth on top.

"Take off that apron, now," she says to me. "There now, go." She hands me the basket and whisks me away. "A man who loves food is a man worth loving."

I don't dare look toward Tattlebug, standing elbow deep in soap bubbles at the sink, for fear her jealous gaze will melt me. I'm sure she is scheming, planning out the when, where, and how she'll tattle to Mackree about Sir Richard. As if Mackree would care. He himself said to find me a prince.

Peter Piper picked a peck of pickled peppers;
A peck of pickled peppers Peter Piper picked.
If Peter Piper picked a peck of pickled peppers,
Where's the peck of pickled peppers Peter Piper picked?

CHAPTER 8

Five-Star Flirting

When I reach the royals' den with the basket, I see the two most handsome PITs of the twelve, Sir Richard the soldier and Sir Peter the pirate, seated at a table staring intently at a chess board. Father taught me the game when I was seven and it fast became one of my favorite sports. I'm a bit of a chess champ. Father hasn't beaten me in years.

I walk close enough to see the carved wood figures, quiet so as not to disturb the play. Sir Richard finishes calculating his options. He lifts a knight and moves it up and over. Sir Peter smiles and quickly sweeps his rook across the board. Oh dear, he's left his queen open to attack.

"Lady Grace," Sir Richard says, looking up. He stands and Sir Peter follows. They move toward me.

Sir Peter nods at the basket. "A present for me?" he says, smiling, crossing his arms over his chest, his silver earring glinting in the candlelight.

Nuff was right. This prince is a looker. And of good humor too.

"No, sir," I say, "sorry. Sir Richard requested this from the kitchen."

Sir Peter chuckles and looks at Sir Richard, impressed with his fellow PIT.

"Thank you, Lady Grace," Sir Richard says, claiming the basket, my eyes, and my attention all at once. He smiles at me, his blue eyes glistening. I feel my face flushing.

"Lady Grace, is it?" Sir Peter says, coming closer.

"Gracepearl," I say.

"A winsome name for a winsome lady," Sir Peter says, bowing with a flourish. "Allow me to introduce myself, Sir Peter of Elmland, at your humble service."

Sir Richard laughs. "Well done, Elmland, charming indeed."

"A pleasure to meet you, Sir Peter," I say with a curtsy, trying to hide a smile. About this, the Muffets seem to know something—*flirting is fun.*

Then I gather my wits back about me. It's late and getting dark. I must go if I want to see Father. "Good evening to you, sirs."

"Wait," Sir Peter says, "stay."

"Yes," Richard says, "our match can wait."

"No, thank you. I really must be off."

Sir Richard follows me into the hallway. "May I call on you?" he says.

Sir Peter comes up beside Sir Richard, slyly dropping the napkin from the food basket on the rug. "You dropped something, Sir Richard," he says.

When Sir Richard looks, Sir Peter leans toward me. "May I call on you?" he says.

Sir Richard snaps the napkin at Sir Peter's head. "Here's a pretty scarf for your ponytail, Peter," he teases. "I know some royal girls who'd give their last glass slipper for such ravishing hair as yours."

Sir Peter roars in laughter. "Yes, Sir Richard, and I know some. . . ."

Two five-star PITs in a verbal joust over me? My head's in a swirl. "I must go," I say. "Good evening."

"Well, my lady?" Sir Richard calls down the hall.

"Well, my lady?" Sir Peter echoes.

I turn and smile, first at one and then the other. "Yes and yes," I say.

They laugh good-naturedly.

"Oh, and, Sir Peter . . ."

"Yes?" he says.

Recalling the positions on the chess board, I know the only way he can spare his queen is to sacrifice his bishop. "I'd pay tithes to the bishop if I were you."

"What?" Sir Peter says, confused.

"The chess game," says Sir Richard, roaring with glee, getting it right away. "So the beautiful Lady Grace is clever too."

Amazed at my new brazenness with boys, I hurry off to the hospital to see Father.

⟡⟡⟡⟡⟡

It is too late. He is asleep. Another nurse, Sister Anne, short and rotund with a pleasant reassuring smile, says that when Doctor Jeffers made his evening rounds "he was quite pleased with Cook's progress."

"Oh, that is good news, indeed, Sister," I say, tears filling my eyes. I clasp my palms together in gratitude. "When he wakes please tell him that his daughter came to visit with her fondest love and that I shall return bright and early tomorrow."

Polly, put the kettle on,
Polly, put the kettle on,
Polly, put the kettle on,
We'll all have tea.

Sukey, take it off again,
Sukey, take it off again,
Sukey, take it off again,
They've all gone away.

CHAPTER 9

The Glory of Girlfriends

I nearly skip away from the hospital I'm so happy to hear Father is on the mend, but the closer to home I get the heavier my heart grows, and my skip slows to a somber trot, dreading the dark and lonely cottage without Father.

Turning the bend, I'm surprised to see a lamp in our front window and another light flickering inside. Lu's face appears in the window. What a nice surprise.

Dear Lu has brought egg salad sandwiches with pickles chopped in the way we both love best, and sweet fried onion chips, succulent strawberries picked fresh from the patch today, a cloth sack filled with warm chocolate cookies studded with walnuts, and her famous sea taffy. And last, but not least, gossip about the princes.

Ahh, the glory of girlfriends.

I take a bite and then another. "It is you who should be the cook one day, Lu. Such talent is wasted cleaning."

"Hmm . . . maybe someday," Lu says.

I try the sweet fried onion chips. "Oh my heavens, these are delicious! "

I was in such a hurry to visit Father, I passed up Nora's spread for the servants. I'm sure she didn't treat the kitchen crew with the pomp and dignity Father always offers on this special evening. She probably fed them in the kitchen instead of insisting they sit in the fine chairs at the royal tables, but nonetheless, I'm sure the food was tasty. No one can say Nora Baker can't cook.

Suddenly ravenous, I devour another sandwich, popping one salty crunchy chip after another into my mouth, washing it all down with fresh sweet lemonade from the jug. Lu laughs, happy to see me eat.

"You're worm thin," she says. "Get some meat on those bones. You'll never fill out a ball gown unless you plump up some."

"You're such a mother, Lu."

"I can't wait to be, someday, Grace. I want to have a

house full of children and a big bright kitchen to . . ."

She stops. Her face clouds. "What, Lu? Tell me," I say.

"My dreams are not meant to come true," Lu says. She turns and begins clearing up from our picnic.

"That's preposterous," I say. "Come here, Lu, right now." I fetch the jewel-rimmed mirror and hold it up to Lu's face. "Look in there," I say.

Lu giggles. "You're silly."

"Go ahead, look," I say.

Lu does.

"Now," I say, "repeat after me. I, Lu."

"I, Lu."

"I, Lu, am beautiful . . . bright and beautiful . . . inside and out."

Lu giggles. She looks away from the mirror. I hold it back up to her face. "Go ahead, say it."

"I, Lu, am beautiful, bright and beautiful, inside and out."

"And the dream I dream will come true."

Lu pauses, then begins to smile. "And the dream I dream will come true."

I grin. "This, I believe."

"Me too, Gracie. This, I believe."

⬦⬦⬦⬦⬦

There's a knock and then the cottage door swings opens. Nuff pokes her head in carrying a blanket and a pillow. "I thought you might like some company tonight."

61

"Come in!" I shout. "Now we're all here."

Lu slides down the couch, making room for Nuff to join us.

I look at them and my heart fills with joy. What would have been a dark and lonely cottage quickly fills to bursting with laughter and good cheer. They are delighted to hear Father is doing better. Talk quickly turns to the PITs.

"I claim Sir Richard the dashing blue-eyed soldier," Lu announces, reaching for a cookie. "I can't stop thinking of him."

A sharp pang of guilt stabs me and I look away so that my face won't betray me. Sir Richard touching my hand in the dining hall, flirting with me in the den just hours ago. "May I call on you?" he asked, and I said yes. In the heady swoon of flattery, I forgot Lu's affection for him. Clearly, from her first sight of Sir Richard on the beach she declared that she was smitten.

Lu's face glows brightly as she babbles on about what she's discovered about Sir Richard. The battles he's fought, the honors he's won . . .

In this moment I resolve to rebuke any further advances from Sir Richard, however handsome and smart he may be. Besides, Gracepearl, remember, it is not romance you seek, but a ship for transport.

There is still Sir Peter, the pirate prince. He is funny and charming and wildly handsome with that long hair in a leather tie, the silver loop glinting at his ear . . .

"How about you, Gracepearl," Nuff says. "What have you learned of the PITs?"

"Wait till you hear about Humpty," I say, telling them how he leered and spoke to me so rudely in the gardens and then destroyed the basket of tomatoes.

"Oh, that won't do," Lu says angrily. "That's no way to treat a lady and no one talks to our Gracie like that. My mum would wash his mouth out with soap."

"Soap could be arranged," Nuff says mischievously. "Or one could tinker with his toothpaste when one cleans his bathing chamber. A little lye would do nicely, I think."

"Humpty Dumpty blowing bubbles!" I say. "That would be fun to see. He had no cause to treat Leem so badly." I smile thinking of how Sir Richard and I spared Leem and his fellow food pirate, Brine, the wrath of Nora Baker at the banquet.

"I heard Leem telling Mum how he rescued Sir Humpty's cap from the water," Lu says. "Leem made Mum swear she wouldn't tell Dad for fear he would punish Leem for embarrassing the family and all of Miramore."

"What!" I say, my voice rising. "What does Leem have to be ashamed of? He acted in a brave and gallant fashion. Tell him I said he's a prince of a boy."

"That's right," Nuff says. "A real prince."

"But how shall we punish Humpty for the tomatoes?" Lu asks, taking another cookie from the sack, brushing crumbs from her lips.

I yawn and Nuff does too, the long day catching up with all of us. "Let's not rush the revenge," Nuff says. "This calls for a truly egg-cellent plan."

Lu and I laugh. Matter settled.

"I saw Mackree today," I blurt out, unplanned. Where did that come from? The workings of my inner mind never cease to surprise me. Like when I hear Mother talking to me as clearly as if we are sitting across from each other in the kitchen having tea.

Lu and Nuff exchange glances.

"And?" Lu says.

"Mackree heard about Father and came to check on me."

"That was thoughtful," Nuff says quietly.

"But that was all. He wouldn't talk to me," I say, emotion rising in a wave inside. "I don't know why he rebukes me. How did I make him hate me so?"

My friends are silent.

"He doesn't hate you, Gracie," Nuff says finally, "you know that."

"But I miss him," I say, tears starting. "I still can't believe he broke off from me."

"Oh, Gracie, dearie," Lu says in a gentle tone. "It was you who ended it."

"No," I say.

"Yes." Lu nods. She touches my arm as if to soften the blow of her truthful words. Nuff squeezes my other arm.

"For a long time now," Lu says, "and more and more it seems this past year, you have been telling all of us about these strange emotions haunting you. The dreams of all the faces and the signs and the guiding words you hear from your mother."

Nuff tilts her head to look in my eyes. "You say you are called to leave Miramore," she says. "Mackree knows he can't go with you. He knows that the only way for you to leave Miramore is with a prince. Mackree could beg you to reconsider, beg you to stay, but his love for you is nobler than that. So he has set you free."

My friends give me time and space to let the pain cry out. After, I wash my face and rejoin them. "Tell me, honestly, are you mad at me for wanting to leave?"

"We're not worried," Nuff says. "We know you'll come back."

"You've always been special," Lu says. "We've always known. Nuff and I, we're content here. You've always wanted something more."

"You'll be the first, Gracepearl," Nuff says with pride in her voice. "The first to marry a prince and leave Miramore."

"Gracepearl the First you'll be," says Lu.

We clean up the crumbs, fold the napkins, and sit back content in silence. Lu begins talking of the gown she's making for the Summersleave Ball. "It's crimson," she says, "like the sunset, and I'm sewing in bits of silver jitties to catch the light."

"I bet Sir Richard will keep your dance card filled all night," I say. "And what about you, Nuff? Has a prince caught your fancy?"

"No, not yet," Nuff says. "I'm still making observations."

Nuff starts a fire in the hearth. I put the tea kettle on. Lu runs home to ask if she can spend the night too. She comes back with a pillow and quilt.

After tea and the last of the good chocolate cookies, arms linked, we walk down to the beach, gazing up at the glittering specks above.

Reaching the water I close my eyes and take a deep breath, sending out gratitude for Father's recovery and these two wonderful friends.

For a few minutes we are each lost in our own reveries, then wishes made, we link arms again and head home, our chatter bubbling fast as a brook.

Back at the cottage we lay out blankets in front of the fireplace and sit together staring at the waning fire, now just glowing embers on a log.

"What about you, Gracepearl?" Nuff asks. "Has a prince caught *your* fancy?"

"Sir Peter interests me some," I say.

Nuff sits back a bit, her body stiffening. I try to catch her eyes, but she won't look my way.

"And you, Nuff," Lu says, "what about you?"

"No one yet," Nuff insists.

I have the sense Nuff is holding back.

"I'm tired," Nuff says, "can we go to sleep?"

"Sure," I say, setting the grate around the hearth.

Lu blows out the candle lamps.

I snuggle beneath my covers. "Good night."

"Good night," Lu answers.

Nuff is silent. Does Nuff fancy Sir Peter?

But Nuff doesn't really even want to marry a prince. She wants to stay on Miramore forever. Surely she won't begrudge me this boy who has a boat I need. There will be other princes for Nuff this year and the next.

I need a boat right now.

A, B, C, D, E, F, G,
H, I, J, K, L, M, N, O, P,
Q, R, S, T, U, and V,
W, and X, Y and Z,
Now I've said my ABC's,
Tell me what you think of me.

CHAPTER 10

"Chop, Chop!"

Dawn blossoms bolder than a fiery orange trumpeter lily on the Isle of Miramore. It begins as a pinkish bud, then blooms and spreads with a wild, unstoppable fury until it basks the entire shore in its glorious glow. Walking the path to the beach, in the distance I faintly hear the guard blowing a wake-up call through a giant whirled queen conch shell to wrestle the sleeping royals from their slumber. It is their first day of summer school.

These privileged young princes attend the finest boarding schools. They are well versed in history, biology, mathematics, and government. They know the intricacies of commerce, the stories of the great leaders of history. They can cite with ease the start and ending days of every major war and the dates of all decisive battles. One among them can even recount the numbers of casualties of both the vanquished and the victorious. But this summer, here on Miramore, none of that knowledge will assist them. This summer they have come to learn another set of talents altogether. Here they will learn, as Lady Jule happily proclaims, what ladies find charming in a gentleman.

Lu and Nuff hurried off to work after I served them a boring bowl of oatmeal. "You really should learn to cook," Nuff had joked. "Why should she?" Lu countered, adding some cinnamon from the cupboard. "Princesses don't need to make porridge."

We made a plan to meet later outside the classroom cottages to begin our annual spying on the royal students.

I gather the vegetables, scoop the coal, and after, as I'm coming up over the bluff, I spot Mackree there below me on the beach.

He is close, but his back is to me. He doesn't realize I am here. There is a large orange and pink speckled crab, shell upturned, rosy-pincered legs scrambling frantically in the air, attempting to turn itself back over before a gull finishes it off. I hear Mackree laugh. He turns the crab over and gently carries it to the water, where it scurry-swims gratefully away.

I smile. That's my Mackree, always quick to help

another, even an ugly old crab. Such a good heart. *My Mackree.* I watch as he picks up a stone and skips it smoothly out over the water. He whistles and walks off. I want so much to call to him, to run and join him on his walk like we've done countless times before. But I stop myself. Mackree did the brave thing of setting me free for another, it is not fair of me to toy with his heart. "You can't expect him to still be your friend," Lu said last night. "It is too painful for him, Gracie."

Lu's right. I will not cause Mackree one more measure of pain. I take a deep breath and let it out and then another and another. I close my eyes. I hear Mother. *Follow your course, Gracepearl my girl. Your inner compass will lead you and then you will choose.*

"Choose what, Mother? Choose what?" I stare out at the rolling waves, whooshing in and out in perfect rhythm. "Rock-a-bye baby on the treetop . . ."

I set off in the opposite direction from Mackree.

My feet lead me to the docks. There is Captain Jessie's ship, sails lowered and tied securely from the wind. I wonder what his business is here? I walk toward the vessel, rub my hand against the wood, a yellowish tan color with dark knots. Pine? Looking to be sure I am alone, I gather my skirts about me and hoist myself on board.

A smile breaks out, my heart beats faster. I'm on a ship! How hard could it be to . . . I sit down and close my eyes. Immediately I see a child. "Help me," she calls. Then she is gone and I see others, so many others, faces young and old. "How?" I call back.

"*Caw!*" A gull swoops near, squawking loudly as if to wake me.

I'm late to meet Lu and Nuff. Classes should be starting now.

✧✧✧✧✧

When I reach the shady knoll where the school cottages are, I see Lu and Nuff hunched beneath the window of Professor Daterly's yellow-shuttered, flower-boxed, bright red cottage. Courtship and Special Occasions. Just then I hear voices and turn to see Sir Richard and Sir Peter walking up from the Royal Lodge, notebooks tucked embarrassedly under their armpits. It seems they've struck up a friendship, these two most princely of all the PITs.

I dodge behind a tree and watch them as they pass. Their faces reveal that they think this class will be a waste of their time and intelligence.

"A class in *dating*?" Sir Richard says mockingly. "I need no such instruction. My degrees in this field are well documented."

Sir Peter laughs. "I'll check you on that, mate. But the . . . *grace*-full girls of Miramore may have something to teach us yet."

I smile at the word "graceful."

71

"Grace-*pearl*-ful, you mean," Sir Richard says, and I nearly giggle aloud.

When they have safely passed me, I run to meet Lu and Nuff. We crouch beneath the classroom window, ears peeled.

"Welcome to Courtship and Special Occasions," Professor Daterly says. "Since the long-standing rules of the Order have changed, no longer requiring or even expecting you royal boys to marry one of your own social class, you now have a much wider, more interesting field of flowers to choose from."

One of the PITs says something and there's laughter. I peek in the window. Sir Humpty Dumpty is clipping his fingernails. He brushes the little arcs on the floor. *Uggh*. I cower back down.

"But this gardening is different, my young royal men," Professor Daterly continues. "In this case, the flower does the picking."

More laughter. "Singe. You just got watered, Humbert."

"That sounded like Sir Peter," Lu says. She sneaks a look in the window. "Yes."

"Does the prince from Elmland have an opinion?" Professor Daterly says, snapping back quickly as garden shears.

"No, ma'am," Sir Peter says.

"Professor Daterly, to you, sir. Now, as I was saying,

much has changed in the world since your great-grandfathers were seeking a match. As you know, historically, royal unions were based on matters of money or land or the military advantage a particular union might create.

"Today you are not bound by such restrictions. You, young men of privilege, you may now marry for love."

"And the *privileges*," Humpty Dumpty shouts.

Big-eared Sir Hickory begins laughing with high-pitched squeals that end in hiccups.

"Muzzle it, mouse," Sir Richard commands good-naturedly, and Sir Hickory does as he's told.

Professor Daterly claps her hands *one, two, three*. "Now then, to our first lesson. The Commandments of Dating. Memorize them. You will be tested tomorrow."

Nuff, Lu, and I roll our eyes. We have heard this lecture countless summers before. I think Professor Daterly is a bit too obsessed with dates, but she is the professor, so who am I to object?

"Certain dates are particularly important," Professor Daterly says. "And, no matter how charming you may be, or how much a girl adores you . . . you will not be forgiven if you forget them.

Nuff pops up for a look. "They're starting to take notes," she reports.

"Number one," Professor Daterly instructs. "Thou shalt remember the date you first met.

"Number two. Thou shalt remember the date of your first date. . . ."

I look at Lu and Nuff, and we cover our mouths to quiet the giggles.

"Number three," Professor Daterly continues. "Thou shalt remember the date of your first kiss."

"Now we're getting somewhere," Sir Peter says, and I can't help but smile. I note Nuff is smiling too.

"Number four. Thou shalt always remember her birth date.

"Number five. Her mother's birth date."

"Excuse me, Professor Daterly," Sir Richard says, "with all due respect. Do girls really care so much about the calendar?"

"See how smart my prince is?" Lu says. I nod in agreement.

"Duck," Nuff whispers. "Professor Pillage is coming."

We hide in the bushes. As he passes, he looks toward the classroom window. "Foolish . . . sissyness . . . waste of time . . . are we teaching mice or men?"

We giggle and take our post again.

I rise up for a peek. "And finally," Professor Daterly says, scanning the faces of her pupils one by one to be sure she has their attention. "The most important date of all. Anyone wish to venture a guess?"

No one does.

"Very well then. Here it is. Thou shalt forever remember your wedding date.

"And"—the professor's voice rises dramatically—"from that day forward, in sickness and in health, in passion and compassion, until death do you part, thou shalt never ever *ever* forget your wedding anniversary—or off to the block you go. Chop, chop." She slices her arm through the air like a carving knife to illustrate the point.

"Chop, chop," I whisper, ducking back down with a laugh, cutting the air with my hand.

"Chop, chop," Nuff says, breaking into a giggle.

"Chop, chop, chop, chop, chop," Lu says, and we run off laughing.

I start and my friends join in,
"Three blind mice, see how they run!
They all ran after the farmer's wife,
She cut off their tails with a carving knife,
Did you ever see such a sight in your life,
As three blind mice?"

"Chop, chop," I mimic again, slicing my hand in the air.

"Chop, chop." Lu chops back.

"When's our anniversary?" Nuff jokes in a taunting tone, hands on hips, lips pursed, head wagging back and forth, feigning anger. "What did you say, boy? The ninth? It's the *nineteenth*, you sorry pimple poke pretending to be a prince. It's the nineteenth, you fool. The *nineteenth*. Do you hear me? You write that date down and memorize it or I'll be getting that carving knife quick. Chop, chop with that crown, chop, chop with that . . ."

"Oh, Nuff," I say, my stomach hurting from laughing. "You are too funny."

"Nothing funny about a carving knife," Nuff says, still in character.

"What's that date?" Lu says.

"The eighteenth?" I joke.

"Chop, chop," Nuff roars. "You're history!"

Hey diddle diddle,
The cat and the fiddle,
The cow jumped over the moon;
The little dog laughed
To see such craft
And the dish ran away with the spoon.

CHAPTER 11

Three Signs

A week goes by and thankfully, Father is well enough to come home. Nora Baker insists I stay home with him, and for that I am grateful indeed.

Lu and Nuff and all of our neighbors bring baskets of food, which takes me off the hook as the cook. Father and I read together. I let him beat me at chess.

Sir Richard comes calling with a bouquet of pink roses. Sir Peter comes calling with a bouquet of red. I speak briefly to each at the doorway, but do not invite them in. I realized I should have kindly rebuffed Sir Richard's gift so as not to encourage his interest, knowing Lu's feelings for him, but my thoughts were ablur. My focus for the moment is Father. The princes will have to wait.

Lu and Nuff come each day for tea and gossip.

"The PITs were comical indeed dancing with brooms and mops in Madame Bella's class," Nuff reports. "Sir Richard swept around the room as if he was star-smitten mesmerized with his raggedy mop. 'Oh my lady, what lovely white locks you have. And what is that sweet perfume? Soap you say? How delightful.'"

Lu and I burst out laughing.

"Then the Muffets pushed open the door," Nuff says, "nearly toppling on the floor, all fancy in dresses and their matching pink shawls."

"How do they get out of work so easy?" I ask.

"This year they'll do anything," Lu explains. "Their mothers cover for them at the mill, so desperate are they for their daughters to marry into money. And I heard Janey Derry boasting that she had the whole summer free from milking too."

"Speaking of Janey," Nuff continues with her story. "She asked Madame Bella if the Muffets could assist with class. 'Surely the princes would prefer beauties to brooms,' she pleaded, batting her doe eyelashes, twirling her frilly parasol. But smart Madame Bella scooted them away. 'You'll have your chance at the ball,' she said."

The only person who does not come to visit me is Mackree. Surely Tattlebug told him about my royal suitors.

◇◇◇◇◇

Waking early, hours before Father, who is such a sleepybear, grumpy if awoken too soon, I head to the beach for my morning walk. Like the forest, the sea has much to teach us, Mother said. "Never miss a chance to walk beside it, daughter, and let its wisdom soothe your soul."

"Hello, Pumpkin," I say to the little orange cat with the striped stumpy tail who saunters out of the brush to greet me. Cats run free all over the island. I've given names and food to many.

Pumpkin purrs and stares at me expectantly.

"Here you go," I say, filling the dish I bring with oats. Pumpkin gobbles it up quick.

Hey diddle diddle,
The cat and the fiddle,
The cow jumped over the moon;
The little dog laughed
To see such craft
And the dish ran away with the spoon.

The rhyme flits in and out again. The cat's green speckled eyes meet mine and I can read the thank you therein. I picture the little girl's face I saw in my mind's eye when I snuck aboard Captain Jessie's boat. She's hungry. That's it.

I pack up the bowl and set off up the beach pondering the meaning of this. I walk briskly, breathing in the good fresh air of a brand-new day. I walk for good health and exercise. I walk with an eye for colorful shells, which I will fashion with string into wind chimes to sell on Trading Day. People favor my sea-chimes very much. I usually sell out by noon. When a good wind blows, you can hear my sea-chimes all over Miramore.

As I walk, I look for signs. Mother said the angels bring us each three signs a day—harbingers of things to come, clues about paths to take, reminders of how precious we are and how very much we are loved.

My gaze is drawn to a small gray rock, standing out from the thousands of pebbles and shells tossed upon the sand. I pick the stone up and study it, appreciating its smoothness and softly curved edges. It resembles the outline of the Madonna and child in the village chapel, the lady's head tilted downward, her arms wrapped protectively around her baby.

I put the first sign safely in my pocket and keep on walking.

The sky is the blue of a robin's egg. The cool waves tease my toes. The sun has cast off the filmy residue of its birth and is now a ball of flame in the heavens.

Thank you, God, for letting Father get better. Please help his heart grow stronger. A traveling band of little sandpipers scampers fast along the beach before me, leaving itty-bitty three-pronged prints in the sand.

Something catches my eye. A second sign. I bend to pick it up.

A small but sturdy branch of pine. The wind must have carried it from the forest, as there are no pine trees such as these by the water's edge. There are two cones attached to the branch. They are connected, married, I think, smiling. I rub the long green needles and touch my fingers to my nose, breathing in the scent that holds such meaning for me.

I stick the second sign in my pocket and continue.

Picking up my pace, pumping my arms, I feel my heart beating strong within. Up ahead a gull nose-dives in and away from a mound on the sand, another gull dives in, then another.

When I reach the mound, I see that it is a mighty silver fish. There is a jagged hole in its side and two gulls are pecking off choice bloody bits for breakfast. As I get closer, the birds squawk angrily off, bothered by my interruption of their morning meal.

I stare at the dead fish's glassy eye. I feel a chill. "No," I say aloud, glad for one simple choice. "That will not be the third sign."

I turn and run up onto the boulders. I hop from rock to rock, out to a place where the waves surround me. I sit on the flat-topped outermost rock and wrap my arms about my knees. I close my eyes, breathe in and out, in and out, feeling the rhythm of the waves, hearing the ocean's voice like a giant snoring, ahh . . . shhh . . . ahh . . . shhh.

The thought of a giant makes me smile.
Fe fi fo fum!
I smell the blood of an Englishman . . .

◇◇◇◇◇

Walking home now, back up the beach, I am drawn to pick up another object. It is a perfectly flat skipping stone. Nothing special about it, except it reminds me of Mackree. How I used to collect bags of these for him. I bring the stone to my lips and kiss it gently.

Into my pocket the true third sign goes. What was that I made Lu and me pledge? Dream a dream and believe it. Design our own destiny. I shake my head. *No, it can't be.*

I hurry home to make tea for Father. He'll enjoy a cup with the honey sweetdrops from Lady Jule.

A man of words and not of deeds
Is like a garden full of weeds.

CHAPTER 12

Coal

On the back step by the dining hall kitchen, I reach for the two buckets and my shovel, then follow the path down to the coal yard, where several others are already gathered for their household's daily allotment.

Greeting Mackree's sister, Laney, and some other early birds, I plunge my shovel into a bin of the dark black chunks and scoop until I fill both buckets to the brim. I swat a fly from my forehead and set off to haul the buckets back up to the kitchen, my arms straining from the weight. A nugget of coal falls to the ground and I stop, set the buckets down, and bend to retrieve it. A nugget of coal is a nugget of gold when you're fueling stoves for cooking.

Nora Baker is looming large in the doorway when I reach the kitchen steps. She wipes her hands on her thick apron, stained with grease from frying bacon, no doubt. I breathe in the pleasant smells of savory meat and eggs and pastries. Compared to my dreadful oatmeal, a breakfast such as that would be lovely indeed.

"There ya are," Nora says, huffing impatiently, pulling the pails with ease from my hands as if they are baskets of feathers. "How's Cook?"

"Better, Miss Nora, thank you." I turn to leave.

"Hold it there, girl. I'll be needing two more today."

I sigh. "Yes, ma'am." I think, Oh please not another trip to the coal yard, but I keep my thoughts to myself.

Nora returns with the empty buckets. I dutifully take them and set off again.

"Hurry back, Gracepearl, and don't be dallyin'," the old cook shouts. "I'll have the garden list waitin' fer ya. And it'll be a long one."

"I'll get right to it, Miss Nora." I'll miss many when I leave Miramore, but I won't miss that battleaxe.

I walk back to the coal yard and wait my turn in the now much longer line. The sun is bright and the buzz of locusts heralds the hot day ahead. There's a volley of laughter and I turn to see a group of PITs heading up the path to Professor Millington's classroom cottage. Some of the princes appear to be practicing a confident swagger as they walk. Sir Humpty stumbles, looks about embarrassed, and then speeds up his canter as if he had been just moving from a walk to a run. Tattlebug has observed the stumble-run and thinks it's funny. She laughs and he sends her a look that could fry an egg.

The princes will be learning Charming Manners today. Sir Richard and Sir Peter walk behind the others, their backs are to me, good thing. I wouldn't want them to see me wearing this ugly smock. For a moment I'm surprised by such feelings. I've never been ashamed of my clothes before my fate hung on my presentation. I might take a clue from the silly Muffets.

Sir Richard turns and gazes over in my direction, and I move quickly to avoid our eyes meeting. When he brought me the roses, I was cool to him. Lu has made plain her interest in Sir Richard, and it would be a breach of our friendship to pursue the solider prince. Sir Peter is a different matter. I have a sense that Nuff likes him. I have made a point of inquiring about Sir Peter, things Nuff may have heard or noticed about the ponytailed prince. I've studied her face for clues as she responded, but if she likes him, she is keeping it a secret. Nuff is my friend and I love her as much as Lu, but until she professes her feelings, the pirate prince must be fair game.

After I present the buckets of coal to Nora, I head to the pump, reaching to rub my aching shoulders, foolishly leaving a black smear on my yellow blouse.

The pump is already well primed, and the fresh cold water fills my washing tub in a few seconds. Reaching for the gritty cake of soap and brush, I scrub the black coal dust from my hands and nails. Coal. Gracepearl Coal. Servants named for the nature of their work. Nora Baker from a line of bakers. Nuff Lundry from a long line of laundresses. Coal for one who digs coal for the kitchens. Gracepearl Coal. It's a nice enough name, the Gracepearl part, that is. If I marry a prince it won't matter anyway. I'll have to take his name. That gives me an unpleasant feeling. Why does a girl have to give up her name? Is a girl's name less important than a boy's? I think not.

Nora is at the door waiting for me with the list of vegetables she needs for today's meals. "Hurry, child. Yer slow as a turtle. I haven't got all day."

"Sorry, Miss Nora. I'll be quick." I take the paper and look it over.

"I want the small red potatoes, eighty of them, no bigger than a silver dollar," the old cook says, circling her thumb and finger to illustrate. "And be sure the green beans are the length of a farmer's finger," Nora instructs with a most serious expression, as if this is a difficult mathematical lesson to grasp.

I stifle a laugh unsuccessfully.

"What?" Nora says sharply.

"It's just I've never heard that rule of measurement before." I giggle. "A farmer's finger. But it is an apt description, Miss Nora, and one I shall duly remember."

I scan down the list, silently noting the misspelled words. Nora Baker never had the benefit of classroom education, but she's a scholar in the kitchen, for sure.

"This long," Nora says, holding her finger up to

demonstrate the bean length again, "but not too bumpy and fat." She smooths her own fat arthritic knuckles to illustrate. "Or the beans'll be dry inside."

"Yes, ma'am," I say. I hook the spade on the loop of my belt, pick up my baskets, and set off to the garden, wishing I was heading to the beach instead. Sir Richard's handsome face flits into my mind. Had he seen me this morning? A cook is one thing, but how would he feel about me as a coal digger? Stop, Gracepearl. Why are you even thinking about Sir Richard? This is so confusing. I sigh angrily and kick a stone.

Mary, Mary, quite contrary,
How does your garden grow?

Hark! Hark! The dogs do bark,
The beggars are coming to town;
Some in rags, some in tags,
And some in velvet gowns.

CHAPTER 13

Confusing Dreams

With a few minutes to spare before I meet Lu and Nuff for lunch, I feel drawn to Mackree's stables. As I come up over the hill, I see him, and take cover behind a tree. He is brushing his prize horse, Ransom.

Mackree's long, dark, rich brown hair blends perfectly with Ransom's mane. Mackree brushes the horse's flanks with long measured strokes, talking to him all the while.

Suddenly Sir Humpty appears, his protruding egg belly clear evidence that he is enjoying our Miramore cuisine. "I'll ride that one in the tournament, boy," he says to Mackree, tapping Ransom's head with a stick.

Ransom rears back. I see Mackree's body stiffen.

"He's taken," Mackree says, not looking up. Mackree coughs and spits.

"Look at me when I talk to you," the egg PIT says.

The barn door swings open and Sir Richard joins them. "Is he ready, Mackree?" Sir Richard asks, nodding toward Ransom.

"Aye, sir," Mackree says, stepping away from his horse.

Sir Richard greets Ransom, then mounts him with ease.

The egg prince is fried. "I claimed that horse," he says to Mackree. "You know that, boy. I'll have you reported."

"I'm no boy," Mackree says in a measured tone. "And good luck reportin'. Ransom is my horse and I'm the only one decidin' who's fit enough to ride him." Mackree spits again.

This time a bit of shiny spittle lands on the egg boy's boot.

"I'll have you whipped," Sir Humbert says, coming toward Mackree with his riding stick raised.

"That's enough!" I shout, rushing forward. "Leave Mackree be, you brute."

Sir Humbert looks at me and laughs. "Well, if it isn't Lady Grace of the Gardens."

"*Uggh*," I sneer at him. "If it isn't the stumbling Humbert."

His smile freezes. He nods at Mackree. "Figures you'd let a girl fight your battles. A real man knows how to . . ." The dining hall bells gong loudly. Humpty's fondess for food rules the day. He leaves, then turns back. "We're not through, *boy*," he says to Mackree. "I would challenge you on Tournament Day, but then, of course, you won't be riding. You'll be scooping dung from my horse's rump."

Mackree moves toward Humbert, but the egg prince hurries off.

I reach to touch Mackree's arm. "What a pompous . . ."

Mackree pulls away like I've stung him. His face is quivering as if he might cry. My heart breaks watching him feel so shamed.

"Go, Pearl, now. *Go*."

And as much as I want to console him, respecting his wishes, I do.

✧✧✧✧✧

Lu and Nuff are waiting for me in the shade of the huckabee tree. Lu offers me a smashed peanut and strawberry sandwich.

"Sir Richard the soldier is such a dearie," Lu says. "Handsome and heartfelt too. How wonderful it would be to wed such a man. When I went to retrieve his chamber pot this morning he said, 'No lady, I'll do that task myself.' Isn't that sweet?"

"And smelly," Nuff says, and we giggle.

"The royals are learning their manners," Nuff says,

separating a segment of juicy orange and popping it into her mouth. "I was walking by the window when Professor Millington was saying how 'ladies are charmed by men with fine manners, especially as displayed at the dining table.'

"She said"—and Nuff hardens her nose, sucks in her cheeks, shoulders back, chin up, affecting the proper posture of the instructor of Manners and Protocol—"'Gentlemen . . . in the presence of a lady, there will be no burping, no slurping, no letting off *steam*—'"

"Steam!?" I nearly choke on my sandwich.

Lu giggles. "What's she mean, steam?"

"Actually I think she said 'bottom steam,'" Nuff answers, "otherwise known as 'gassy vapors.'"

"Oh, Nuff," I say, "enough. You are too *too* funny."

"Bottom steam?!" Lu repeats. "Oh, no, she didn't say that."

"Did too," Nuff says, waving her hand in front of her nose, and we three double over laughing.

I notice Nuff instinctively puts her hand over her mouth to cover the broken front tooth she thinks makes her unattractive. That, of course, is silly. Nuff is beautiful, especially when she's laughing. But you can tell a person something a million times and that doesn't make it true for them unless they feel it inside. Unlike Lu and me, Nuff is more private about her feelings. I recall how silent she became when talk turned to Sir

Peter that night at my cottage. I wonder if she likes him. No. I would have picked up something by now. Tattlebug's been gushing waterfalls of PIT gossip—who was seen walking with whom, who was seen talking with whom, and while she's often mentioned "Moo-Lu's moon eyes for Sir Richard," she hasn't said a word about Nuff, nor have I heard her mention either of my prospects.

"Well, that's all fine and dandy that the princes are learning some manners," Lu says. "I hope they take good notes." She tucks a lock of her lovely red curls behind her ear. "But I'm in charge of cleaning those royal boys' bedrooms and I say the lot of 'em, 'cept a few, oughtta be sent back to nursery for some training in aimin'."

"Say what?" Nuff says.

"The half of 'em can't aim their pee in the pot."

Nuff and I burst out laughing.

"That's not very nice, Lu," I say.

"Nothing nice about wiping up pee neither," Lu says, swishing away the last of the creamy peanut and strawberry sandwich crumbs from her lap. "You're lucky you don't have brothers, Gracie."

Lu has four of them. Nuff has two.

"A brother would have been nice," I say. "A sister too." I look from Nuff to Lu. "But, then again, I've got two sisters right here."

"That's right," Nuff says.

"For always," Lu agrees.

"Have you heard any gossip about Captain Jessie?" I ask.

"Not a word," Nuff says.

"Me neither," Lu says. "But enough of that old goat, let's talk about the ball! My aunt Lisha gave me a pair of red shoes that match my gown perfectly. What are you wearing, Nuff?"

"The same blue dress as last year, just sewing in some shiny bits about the hem."

We lie back on the soft grass to rest before afternoon chores. The day is warm and it is quiet. Sleep sweeps over me.

I am standing by Captain Jessie's boat, staring out at the waves, foaming as if a storm approaches. Could I sail this myself? I wonder. Can I really leave Miramore? But then there's the shoals and fiery whirlpools. I sit on the sand to think. I lie back and close my eyes. As soon as I do, I see the faces.

"Here I come," I say, and now I am floating cloud high in the sky, beneath the flapping wings of a giant gray gander, suspended from her beak by two shiny ribbons in a purple-rimmed clamshell with dainty ridges, arms wrapped about my knees tucked to my chest, rocking ever so gently, peaceful and safe. *Will you heed the call, Gracepearl,* Mother asks, her voice so close I can nearly touch her. *This birthday, the gift will surprise you, my dear* . . .

"Mother, where are you, what do you mean?" And then she is gone and the goose is singing, "Rock-a-bye baby, on the treetop, when the wind blows the cradle will rock, when the bough breaks the cradle will fall, and down will come baby, cradle and . . ."

"Ahh!" I sit up, shaking, a cold sweat on my forehead.

"What is it, Gracie?" Lu asks, waking too, touching my arm.

"A nightmare?" Nuff says.

"No," I say, "just too many confusing dreams."

I had a little pony,
His name was Dapple Gray;
I lent him to a lady
To ride a mile away.
She whipped him, she slashed him,
She rode him through the mire;
I would not lend my pony now
For all the lady's hire.

CHAPTER 14

Taming Onions

When I report to the kitchen for my afternoon duties, Nora Baker is ready and waiting, no "hello" or "how was your lunch," just a hurried nod toward the pile of onions on the counter. "There ya go, girl."

Oh, no. Not the onions. They make my eyes cry so. Father always spared me this least favorite of the kitchen tasks. I rinse off my hands, roll up my sleeves, sigh a loud sigh, and begin. Picking up a fat yellow onion, I peel away the shiny skin, crinkling my lashes, bracing myself for the sting. Sure enough, just as I slice it in half and then quarters, my eyes burn and my nose leaks like a spigot.

Tattlebug sneezes loudly at the sink, sending soap bubbles everywhere.

"Shove a hunk of bread in your mouth," Nora shouts over to me from the table where she's gutting a fresh catch of shark, blood smattering everywhere.

"What," I ask, sniffling.

The old baker turned head chef rolls her eyes as if I'm dimwitted. "The bread will soak up the stinging airs," she says. "Never let an onion take ya down, girl. Gotta learn to tame it."

I smile thinking how I'll tell Lu and Nuff about this bit of wisdom. I wipe my eyes on my sleeve, cut off a piece crust from the loaf, and stick it in my mouth. Feeling foolish, but hopeful, bread hanging from my lips, I reach for another onion. I peel it and halve it and quarter it, and like magic, this time my eyes don't water.

"Fank you, Miff Mora," I say, my words muffled in the soggy bread. What a smart idea. I make a mental note to ask about the science behind this phenomenon when school with Lady Jule resumes in September. But then I won't be here in September. Summer days are slipping away. If Sir Peter is the prince for me, I must step up my pursuits . . .

"Aye," Nora says, the faintest hint of a smile the only indication that she heard the compliment in my thanks.

Later I steal a closer look at the old woman's nearly always stern face. Nora Baker has plump cheeks and hazel eyes, her thick gray, white-streaked hair hangs down her back in a braid, nearly long enough to sit on, with just a few raven strands as evidence of the color it once was. As she deftly scales and bones another fat gray fish, scraping the waste into a pile, later to be tossed in the mulch bin, Nora seems to forget the rest of us working beside her in the kitchen. Her face takes on a soft, tranquil expression.

She looks happy, I think. That's it. She is doing work she loves. To me, kitchen work is drudgery. To Nora, kitchen work is joy. How different we all are. Each with different gifts. What is mine, I wonder. All I know for certain is that I'm to find out somewhere other than Miramore.

⬦⬦⬦⬦⬦

Later, after dinner, Father suggests a game of chess.

"How are you doing, daughter?" he says, lining his pawns in a row.

"Fine," I say, lining up mine, wanting to say much more, but not wanting to burden him in his sickness and uncertain of how he will react to my strange and haunting calling. I long to tell him of this anxiousness, how I love Mackree but instead have been flirting with princes, and then there are the faces that . . .

My hand freezes on the last pawn as I fight back tears.

"Gracepearl," Father says, covering my hand with his grand one. "Talk to me. How can I help?"

There is a knock at the door. Mr. Sparks, the candle maker, one of Father's best chums. "Welcome," I say. "Do come in. Father will be much cheered to see you."

I head outside. The garden's in full bloom. I gather some blue lilybells, purple and pink asters, and three sprigs of Queen Anne's lace and bring them inside to find a ribbon and a basket. Mackree's mother's birthday is this week, I know. Mrs. Byre has always been kind as a mother to me and I have missed her lately. I call in to tell Father where I'm going.

"Be home before dark," he says.

Hopefully Mackree will be out in the stables, far enough away from his cottage to even know I am visiting. When I come up over the hill to the Byres' horse farm, I hear galloping and then there's a whirl of dust as Sir Humpty races past me on Mackree's prized steed. The egg-shaped PIT strikes the muscled stallion's glistening brown coat with his long black rod.

"Charge! Charge! We shall be victorious!" he shouts, digging his heels in roughly. He is bouncing up and down like he's taming a wild colt rather than riding a prize-winning Thoroughbred. *Fall off and crack,* I yell in my mind.

Humpty whips the horse again. "Charge!"

Fool. Cruel fool. I have half a mind to shout to him. There is no need to beat Ransom. Mackree already said that Sir Richard will ride Ransom in the tournament, and the finest horse on Miramore needs no rod to win a race. Mackree would be furious if he knew. But I won't intercede and shame Mackree again. Sometimes it's so hard to know what to do.

Frustrated, I turn toward Mackree's cottage. When I reach the porch, my breath catches in my throat. Nuff is sitting with Mrs. Byre.

Mrs. Byre pours Nuff a cup of tea. Nuff says something and they laugh, so familiar, like old friends or family. Since when does Nuff visit my Mackree's mother? Maybe this is why she was so oddly quiet that night by the fire. Maybe it's not Sir Peter that Nuff is fond of. Maybe it is Mackree! My heart is pounding. My stomach churns. What is wrong with you, Gracepearl? You should be happy. If Nuff likes Mackree, then you are free to pursue Sir Peter without concern. Mackree said he would seek a girl who was happy living on Miramore. Nuff is that for certain. And see how kind and beautiful she is. Why wouldn't Mackree be charmed by her?

"Gracepearl!" a man's voice calls, and I turn.

Mr. Sparks, the candle maker, huffing and red-faced, is hurrying toward me.

My heart stops and starts again. Father.

I drop the basket. "The hospital?"

"Yes," he says. "Not to worry. I'm sure he will be fine. Just a bit of indigestion is all."

Bobby Shaftoe's gone to sea,
Silver buckles on his knee;
He'll come back and marry me,
Pretty Bobby Shaftoe.

CHAPTER 15

A Miramore Moonlight Sonata

Reaching the solemn building faster than I would on Ransom's back, I yank open the heavy door, scrunch my nose at the medicine smell, and race to the room where Father was last time.

His face is pale as flour, his breathing faint as a kitten's. I cup my hand to my mouth to stifle a sob, and fall into the chair next to his bed.

After a long while, Father opens his eyes. His smile is the sun winning over a storm cloud.

"Gracepearl, my love," he says quietly. He inches his large frame upward with labored effort and a grimacing wince.

I lean in. He wraps me in his arms.

"Now, now," says the gnome-faced Nurse Hartling, sailing swiftly into the room. "Let's try to keep our patient calm, young lady. Cook is stable now. Let's keep it that way." She looks at Father and—wait, is that a small smile on that usually stern face?

No surprise though, really. Wherever Cook Coal is, it is merrier.

"What happened, Father?" I say.

"I'm fine. Doctor said it was indigestion."

"Oh, thank goodness," I sigh, relieved.

Nurse Hartling clears her throat, wanting me to go. I want to tell Nurse Hartling to go, but remembering the power of honey, I say, "Yes, Nurse, of course, you know best."

The nurse's thin lips pucker into another smile. "It's late, but I will give you a few minutes." She touches her cap and adjusts the collar on her dress. "I'm off to my other patients now. I have some sixteen to attend to, you know."

"Oh, sixteen? That is very many patients indeed," I say.

Father winks ever slightly, just for me to see.

At the door, Nurse Hartling turns back, unable to resist her nature. "Just a short visit," she says to me. "Cook needs his rest."

When she leaves, Father smiles broadly and mimics my earlier comment about Nurse Hartling's patients. His eyes are bright and happy. "You've got your mother's sweet way with words you do. And her beauty. And her heart."

Father and I visit for a bit. I am sure he is getting better and he will come home with me soon. Leaving the hospital, I take a deep breath of sweet island air. Captain Jessie, where has that man been, passes me on the path. We exchange greetings. What a curious man. I wonder what he's up to? I turn as if I'm going into the chapel and when it's safe I take a peek back up the road just as Captain Jessie is entering the hospital.

Hmm. Interesting. Maybe he likes Nurse Hartling. The thought of that makes me laugh. Feeling happier now that I know Father is okay, I head home with a hopeful heart.

There is something on my front step. As I approach I see it is the birthday basket for Mrs. Byre that I dropped when I hurried off to see Father. The flowers are wilted now. Who brought this? Nuff? Mackree? My head is swirling with so many confusing emotions. Enough of this. I cannot care about these Miramore matters. Clearly Mackree has moved on and I must too. It is a prince I need. A prince and passage to the world that calls me.

Sir Peter. I will find Sir Peter this instant. I'll not sit idle on a tuffet waiting for him to come calling again. This time, I will take charge of my destiny.

◈◈◈◈◈

Sir Peter seems stunned but delighted to see me outside his lodge.

"Lady Grace," he says, bowing his head slightly, a smile springing to his lips. "To what do I owe this most welcome surprise?"

"Will you walk with me?" The words rush out like a gale of wind.

The smile leaves his face for a second and when it returns, there is a sweet joy in his eyes to match. "Gladly," he says, offering me his arm.

I hear a rustle in the bushes. Tattlebug, no doubt.

"Gracepearl," he says. "May I call you that?"

He looks so dashing in the moonlight. "Yes, of course." I nod my head.

"And you must call me Peter."

"Peter," I say, "of course."

We walk toward the beach. A breeze wafts by us, setting two sets of my sea-chimes on nearby cottage doorways tinkling.

"How lovely," Peter says, "like music." He stops and reaches out to touch one of the chimes. "I've never seen anything like this before."

"I made it," I say.

He looks into my eyes and smiles. "And so your list of talents grows. I'd much prefer this music to the lutes and pipes I must endure at home."

"Thank you," I say.

"Could I impose on you to make one for me?" Sir Peter asks.

"You can purchase one tomorrow at Trading Day," I say. "I have a booth."

"And the lady is skilled at commerce as well?" He laughs. "Lady Grace, you are delightful. So absolutely refreshing."

I think I hear the telltale sneeze of Tattlebug. "Let's keep walking," I say.

Soon we reach the beach.

"I came to visit you earlier," Sir Peter says. "Your father was being carried off on a stretcher and I couldn't discover where you were. The nurse at the hospital, a tight one she is, wouldn't let me enter without family permission, prince or no prince she said . . ."

I laugh. "That would be Nurse Hartling. She could use a charm class herself."

Sir Peter laughs, relieved that I am laughing. He looks up toward the heavens.

"Such a beautiful night," he says. "Too perfect to waste on sleep. Miramore is a paradise. I could get used to living here." He stands there looking out at the water.

I think of Nuff, how they would make a winsome pair, then I think of the faraway faces, still calling out in my dreams. I glance up at the squid ink sky, vanilla cookie moon, sugar-speckle stars glistening. Just now, one star leaps toward another. The wind blows. It is so romantic here.

"Yes," I say. "The night is grand. Too lovely to waste on dreams."

The pirate prince smiles a smile that could melt a chocolate bar. He bows, then extends his bended arm forward, his eyes never leaving mine. "A dance, my lady," he says.

I curtsy. "My lord."

We dance as if we are royalty. A picture wafts into my mind. I am processing into a grand ballroom, not the modest one here on Miramore used once a year for the Summersleave Ball, but a golden grand ballroom in a regal palace. There is a man, his back is to me, dressed in royal garb, standing alone at the bottom of the staircase. I try to see his face, but he turns from me. Who is he?

Shaking off this vision, I look at the very real Sir Peter. How dashing he is in his wild sea-tossed hair and silver loop. *Pretty Bobby Shaftoe's gone to sea, silver buckles on his knee . . .* A silly child's nursery rhyme.

I am no longer a child. Tonight I feel very grown-up.

"I understand your birthday approaches," Peter says. "August tenth, yes?"

"Very good, Peter. Professor Daterly would be pleased."

He laughs, and I do too.

"I thought you were older," Sir Peter says. "And I mean that as a compliment. You seem wiser than sixteen, so much more mature than those flitty pink girls."

"The Muffets?" I say.

"The Muffets?" He laughs. "That's perfect. The Muffets have surely mastered how to chatter and flatter a man, but I search for a wife who will be my equal. I desire a mate, not a muffet."

His words waltz through my mind as we dance. I imagine boarding Sir Peter's ship in September, the wet sea breeze on my face . . .

"Achoo." The telltale sneeze of Tattlebug lets me know we are not alone.

But I will not let her occupy my mind. Just for this moment, I will not worry about a thing. I breathe in the citrus scent of the larabond trees, hear the wind whistling like piper flutes through the leaves, and now the strong drumbeat of the surf, wave cymbals clashing against the rocks . . . Ahhh, shhhhm . . . ahhh, shhhm, a Miramore moonlight sonata . . . just for this prince and me.

Rub-a-dub-dub,
Three men in a tub,
And who do you think they be?
The butcher, the baker,
The candlestick maker;
And all of them went to sea!

CHAPTER 16

Mermen

The next morning as I return from my early walk on the beach, three treasures—a quill feather, a fishing hook, a silver spoon with lacy holes burned through from the salt water—in my pocket, I pluck a callaberry flower, stick it behind my ear, and turn up the bend to my cottage.

Sir Richard is walking toward me. He nods his chin upward. Clearly he is coming to call. He has seen me—I can hardly pretend to be away.

His eyes are a startling deep-sea blue, his handsome face freshly shaven. There's a scent of lime about him. Wearing swimming shorts, he is shirtless, a towel draped carelessly over his broad shoulders.

"Good morning, Lady Gracepearl," he says with a

107

bow, a wide smile flashing to display perfectly straight white teeth. His eyes scan my face and hair, the red callaberry flower, settling on my eyes. His look is so intense, I look away, then back again.

"Just when I am certain I have seen the most beautiful sight on this isle of paradise, I am even more enraptured," Sir Richard says.

My face blushes in the glow of his praise, in spite of my good friend's heart.

"It seems the fine gentleman from Ashland has no need of the course in flattery this summer."

Sir Richard laughs. "And I see the fine flowers of Miramore have voices and wits to match."

I smile. "How are you finding your stay here, Sir Richard?" I say, trying to steer the conversation in a more formal direction. With Nuff and Mackree, and Lu's claim to Sir Richard, I can focus on Sir Peter and hurt no one.

"Better by the minute," he says, "but, please, call me Richard."

"And the classes," I say, "how go they?"

"Professor Quill nearly puts me to sleep droning on about love letters, sonnets and poems, etcetera, etcetera."

I laugh.

"Is it true ladies are so charmed by the turn of a candied phrase?"

"I suppose it depends on the lady," I say, "and the phrase. And the candy."

"Well done." Sir Richard laughs. "And what of you, Gracepearl? What sort of sweets do you favor?"

"Chocolates and nut crunches, honey-drops, mint wellups, and sea taffies . . ."

"Ah, yes." Sir Richard smiles. "A pretty girl leaves sea taffies on my pillow when she cleans my room."

"That's Lu!" I say. Oh, yes, good. "My friend Lu. Isn't she beautiful? And so kind. And oh what a cook. The sea taffies are just one of her specialties. She makes them herself. And such a good heart. She would do anything to help another. That's my friend Lu. Beatiful inside and out—"

"I came to ask if you would care to join me for swim," Sir Richard says, interrupting me.

"No thank you, Sir . . . Richard. I am not dressed for the occasion."

The sound of male voices and laughter swells up over the cliff from the beach below. Richard turns toward the noise and with a look of reluctance says, "Well then. Maybe we shall meet again tonight. I hear there is a bonfire and dancing in the woods."

"Yes. I'll be coming with my friends Lu and Nuff. I'd like you to meet them, especially Lu."

"Yes, Lady Lu," he says. "She of the sweet taffies?"

"That's right." I start to walk away and then turn back. "Do you want to have a big family someday, Richard? With lots of children?"

He laughs. "The more the merrier. Why do you ask?"

"No reason." I smile, thinking of Lu. "I am not sure what I want."

Sir Richard raises his eyebrow, and I add quickly, "Be careful of the sun, my lord. You wouldn't want to burn at the height of summer."

Laughing and shaking his head, he's off down the pathway to join the other PITs.

I race to Lu's cottage, where she's just waking up. "Hurry," I say, filling her in.

We run to Nuff's cottage and Lu calls her to join us. "Nuff, posthaste. The PITs are swimming!"

✦✦✦✦✦

The sounds of shouting and laughter rise up loud as we approach the shore.

"I wonder, does Sir Peter keep his hair tied or let it hang loose like a merman," I say. Nuff casts me an odd look, then shrugs her shoulders.

"Do you think Sir Richard has a hairy chest?" Lu gushes, blushing.

"What I wonder," Nuff says, "is does Humpty Dumpty boy swim or just float like a hardboiled egg?"

We giggle and duck under the branches of the scrubby beach trees, inching our way out to a secluded ledge where we will be able to perch and see the princes swimming without them seeing us.

Mackree and I used to come here. Last Hallow's Eve he tried to kiss me. I was startled. I giggled, turning my cheek away. Then, at the Christmas Eve dance in the woods, he pulled me close, trying to kiss me again, but I twirled away. "Silly boy." I would not push Mackree away now. No, Gracepearl, it is over. I force my mind to silence my heart.

Lu is the first one to reach the ledge. "Ahhh!" she gasps.

Nuff is the next one out. "Oooh!" she says.

"What? What?" I say, finally edging out.

I look down, the scene below me coming into focus.

The PITs are swimming, frolicking like seals. One ducks another's head underwater to what seems will be the point of drowning, but then the dead-head bobs up and spits and coughs, and arms lunge back to return the favor.

"What's wrong?" I say. "They look like they're having fun."

"Wait," Lu says, "watch."

The royal boys, usually so given to pomp and circumstance and rules and protocol are, here in the sea, playful as nursery boys, carefree as mermen.

There is Sir Richard. He dives down and flips up. Wait. Was that his bum? Lu and Nuff giggle. I saw myself just moments ago he was wearing swimming shorts. A gull caws and my eyes follow the bird to where it alights on a large boulder draped with towels. Towels and shirts and shorts. Oh dear!

"The PIT from Maple is swimming in," Lu says. "Marcus, his name is."

When Sir Marcus reaches shore he stands and we nearly fall off the ledge.

This prince is wearing nothing but his birthday suit and he's wearing it quite well.

"Grace," Lu says, "did you by chance bring your spyglass?" We all laugh.

"I've got an idea," Nuff says. "A naughty idea. Come on!"

We follow her from the ledge, back through the brush and around down to the boulder where the PITs' clothes are strewn. "Blame the laundress in me," Nuff says, laughing mischievously, "but clothes tossed in a heap must be on their way to washing, right?" She starts scooping up the PITs' things.

"Come on," Nuff says. "What are you waiting for?

"I don't know," Lu says, ever the more cautionary one. I think of her sea taffy presents to Richard, surprised at her secret boldness.

"Let's do it," I say. "A little joke never hurt anyone."

◇◇◇◇◇

It was easy to spot Sir Humpty's apparel, being of a certain extra-rotund girth, and while we safely deposited the other PITs' shorts and towels, folded nicely in a spot up the beach where they could easily find them, as Nuff had suggested, we had taken our time in finding a good revenge for what he did to Leem on the beach and me in the garden, and now a truly perfect method had presented itself. We added a bit, well, to be honest, more than a bit, of poison-ivy itching powder to his preposterous pink and yellow flowered undershorts.

"He'll be scratching his shell all week," Nuff said. "Just wait. You'll see."

"I think I'd rather not," I say, laughing.

"You two are wicked." Lu shakes her head. "Wonderfully wicked."

The Queen of Hearts,
She made some tarts
All on a summer's day.
The Knave of Hearts,
He stole those tarts
And took them clean away.

CHAPTER 17

Trading Day

The sky is gray and heavy with clouds on Trading Day. Hopefully the rain will hold back until after I've sold my sea-chimes. There are twenty at least, this month, with colorful shells of various shapes and sizes, from the delicate yellow periwinkles to the thick purple whirled sunsprays. I look for shells with holes bored through them and then I string and knot and arrange them. The right combination makes a sweet melody when they meet in midair.

Checking to be sure the knots are secure, I slide my chimes on a long pole and set off for the square, proud of my work. I am early, but Nora Baker and Tattlebug are there setting out pastries and pies and tarts. I wave and continue down to my stall. I pull back the tarp, brush off my counter, and hang the chimes along my display rope. They look like mermaid necklaces. I smile to myself. With wind they'll sing the music of the sea.

Soon Nuff will be here with her mother selling soaps and lotions, healing potions and perfumes. Sally Tailor will assist her mother selling dresses. Janey Derry and her mother sell eggs and butter. I am the only Miramore girl to have her own booth. It took two years to convince Mooney, the growly man who runs Trading Day, but when he saw what a draw my chimes were as I sold them displayed on a blanket on the hill near the edge of the stalls, I think he calculated the commissions he was losing and finally saw the wisdom of a new way.

"When money talks, Mooney listens," Father said with a chuckle. If only I could succeed at convincing dear Lu to approach him about sharing her sweets with a booth of her own. But she fears disappointing her family with such public dreams of other trades.

Soon the square is filled with Miramores coming to purchase and trade. Spirits are high, as this is a day we all look forward to. A mop of Muffets stroll by stuffing their mouths with cream cups and savory tarts. They whisper and roll their eyes at me. They don't think a girl should be running a business. I turn away to adjust one of my chimes. "When's she going to act like a lady," I hear one of them say.

My face reddens, from anger, not shame. I'm about to say something, but then I see Sir Richard approaching.

"Lady Gracepearl," he says, bowing. The Muffets stop and stare.

"Sir Richard," I say with a curtsy.

The Muffets' antennae have perked up. They are coming toward us.

"Is this your handiwork, Lady Grace?" Sir Richard says, reaching out to touch first one chime and then another. "I've never seen such whimsical ornaments, and what lovely sounds they make."

Before I can answer, one of the Muffets, Chappy Lure, a fisherman's daughter, says, "Oh look, girls, come see Grace Coal's new shell thingies. Aren't they sweet?" And then all the pink-shawled spiders are swarming in front of my stall, making believe they are looking at my sea-chimes when they're really trying to snatch up the prince.

"Well, look what the wind blew in," I say under my breath.

Sir Richard hears me. He bursts out laughing. "Oh lady, you slay me, you do."

And then Sir Peter is there too. Good.

"Here you are, Lady Gracepearl," he says, a wide grin on his face. "The busiest spot on the square, no surprise. I've come to buy your wind chimes, the whole store please."

"Now wait just a moment, Peter," the soldier prince from Ashland says. "You'll have to wait in line. I was here first."

The Muffets are shocked, heads turning back and forth amongst themselves, to the princes and me. They know I've never been very interested in the summer royals before—they must not have believed Tattlebug's rumor about my quest for a prince.

Nuff rushes up to whisper in my ear. "Listen," she says, and then can't go on she's laughing so hard. "Sir Humpty . . ."

I giggle and she giggles. "Oh, Gracie," she says, cupping her hands about her mouth by my ear. "The egg prince just came to Mother's stall looking for bum balm."

"Bee balm?" I say, thinking of the lip-soothing salve Nuff's mother fashions from the wax of bees.

"Shh!" Nuff doubles over laughing again and then regains herself, whispering in my ear again. "*Bum* balm, Gracie. *Buttocks* balm. It seems the prince from Oakland acquired a most unusual island rash."

"Oh, no," I say. "Not the dreaded Miramore 'gotchagood' weed? I hope you warned good Sir Humbert to exercise more caution as he gets 'the lay of the land,' so to speak."

"*Hmm, hmm.*" Sir Peter clears his throat. I note that he and Nuff lock eyes for a moment. She looks away, and so do I.

"Later, Grace," Nuff says, a solemn tone now in her voice. "Mother needs me." I notice Mackree strolling down the hill toward the market, and I wonder if Nuff saw him too. Maybe he comes to buy some of her mother's special lotions for his horses. I shake my head and turn back to the princes as Nuff returns to her booth.

"How much for the store?" Sir Richard says.

I smile.

"Whatever the cost, I'll double that," Sir Peter says.

The Muffets make twittering sounds.

I look at my chimes.

I look at the princes.

I see Mackree approach Nuff's stand.

"What do you want them for?" I ask.

The two five-star PITs regard me carefully.

"To brighten the dreary halls of Elmland," Sir Peter says.

"To share with the sick of Ashland, so the music might help them heal," Sir Richard counters.

You win this one, Sir Richard, I think. What a noble response. If Lu wasn't so enamored of you . . . But no, I will not allow myself to continue the thought.

"Music to my ears, fine sirs. You shall each have an equal share."

Lavender's blue, dilly dilly,
Lavender's green;
When I am king, dilly dilly,
You shall be my queen.

CHAPTER 18

Heart to Heart with Father

Hauling the pails of coal to the kitchen I think of the dance in the woods tonight and then of the Summersleave Ball next month. "Lavender's blue, dilly dilly, lavender's green. When I am king, dilly dilly, you shall be my queen." This year I will wear my new purple satin dress to the ball. Mother's letter directed Father to give it to me on my fourteenth birthday. It was way too big for me then. It fits me perfectly now. I'll wear my oyster shell necklace from last birthday and weave a callaberry and Queen's Lace crown.

Alone on the garden path, I begin to skip. Imaging the music I will hear tonight in the circle in the woods, my feet step to the rhythm, I whirl and twirl. I am happiest when I am dancing, when all confusion slips away.

I gather the lettuce, cucumbers, tomatoes, and beets, then hurry to the kitchen, where Nora greets me with today's next assignment. Peeling potatoes. Mounds of potatoes. I set my knife to the mottled brown skin of the first ugly spud and begin. My thoughts soon return to dancing, and then to my behavior yesterday, in equal measure.

I think of how the Muffets seem to live all year for the Summersleave Ball. Hoping a prince will fall in love with them, maybe even profess his love at the ball. So many silly school stories and plays have this same exact plot. A handsome prince comes for summer study in the charming arts, meets a beautiful Miramore girl, a Muffet, of course, offers her a ring at the Summersleave Ball before a jubilant crowd and then the couple sails away to some far-off castle, where they will marry and live happily ever after.

And now such a fairy tale could turn true. "You could be the first," Nuff had said. I might sail away from Miramore in mere months. Then I think of the glance she and Sir Peter exchanged at Trading Day. Could it have meant that there is nothing between her and Mackree? My heart speeds up.

My heart is pounding. It's as if a fog is lifting and I can suddenly see clearly. I look down at the ugly potato peels and laugh. Tattlebug peers over at me. How is it that now, in this seemingly unimportant moment, in this kitchen, peeling potatoes, how do I know what my heart has decided? My eyes fill with tears, happy tears. My calling to leave Miramore is strong, and yet my tie to Mackree is unbreakable. To leave him would leave half of my heart on this island.

Purl Will U Maree Me? Mackree had written in the sand that day.

"Yes!" I say aloud.

Tattlebug is staring at me. "Who ya talking to?"

"No one," I say. "Mind your beeswax."

Mackree's face appears in my mind. Mackree, who makes me light up like a thousand stars born all at once of a night while the fiddle music weaves magic and the cow jumps over the moon. And yet my mind tells me I must go. My mind says my heart must be silent. I ache now knowing why it pains Mackree to see me. Maybe I can spare myself some sorrow too by avoiding him as much as I can until I leave Miramore. But how can I leave on a boat with a boy who may well be the heart's desire of one of my best friends? Oh, this is heart-boggling brain-wrenching confusing . . .

◆◆◆◆◆

When I am finally done in the kitchen, I hurry to the hospital to visit Father.

Good news, he's been released.

"Thank the heavens," I say, throwing my arms around a startled Nurse Hartling and rushing off home.

I enter the cottage quiet as a mouse so as not to wake Father should he be sleeping. There he is, sitting up in bed, writing. He pauses, reads over what he's written, dips the quill feather in the ink pot and continues. For some reason I know not to disturb him. I wait outside his room. When I look back in, he is stuffing the paper, looks like several pages, into a thick red volume. I recognize it is the book of history Mother taught me from. How odd. Father closes the book, a sweet-sad smile on his face. He sets the book down and picks up the pine pillow I gave him as a child. He brings the pillow to his nose and sniffs, breathing it in and out, tears now rolling down his cheeks.

"Father?"

"Gracepearl." He sniffs and wipes his cheeks with the back of his hand. He smiles. "Come sit beside me. Tell me all your news."

"No, Father, tell me of you. Are you all right?"

"Yes, Gracepearl. I am fine. It will make me happy to hear of you."

Tell Father about the dreams, I hear Mother speak inside me.

"Mother talks to me always," I blurt out.

"Yes," Father says, smiling, "to me as well." He pats the spot beside him and I sit.

"Just this morning Miriam reminded me that your sixteenth birthday fast approaches, as if I would forget."

Suddenly I am wary of this next birthday gift. I am curious, but afraid. The spyglass, the mirror, the necklace, the purple dress . . . the presents have always been perfectly lovely, but Mother has said this year's gift will be different from the rest. Suddenly I do not want my birthday to come. "Maybe we should skip the present this year," I say.

A sadness washes over Father's dear face and just as quickly he covers it with a smile. He reaches out to touch my hair. "Miriam and I talk often of our beautiful girl all grown up. We could not be more proud, Gracepearl. You are all that we dreamed of in a child, way beyond our wildest imaginings."

Tears well up in my eyes. "Father, I love you so." I hug him.

"You have brought me so much joy," he says.

"You sound like it's ending," I say. "We will always be together."

"In spirit, yes child," he says. "Forever heart to heart."

"You're getting better, Father," I say, voice rising. "Look, you're home now and the color has returned to your cheeks. You have years to . . ."

"Gracepearl," he says, his face moving with what seems like so many conflicting emotions. "This birthday . . . the gifts . . . they will be different from the others."

"*Gifts*, Father? I don't understand."

"I wish I could have prepared you more."

"Prepared me for what, Father?"

"Ahhhh. . . ." He lets out a long sweet sigh. "I promised your mother to wait until your birthday. We made a pact and I have faithfully followed her wishes."

"I grow to dread this birthday," I say. I feel now that I must tell Father of my confusion. "Mother speaks of a destiny, a calling. Of a choice I will make. I think of leaving Miramore, but how? The only way is to marry a prince, and yet my one true love is Mackree. And I am haunted by these strange and recurring dreams . . ."

"What dreams? Tell me."

"People," I say. "Hundreds, thousands, old and young, never the same faces . . . they look beaten down, hungry, sad . . . they beckon to me, call me, come, come. Oh Father, what do they want?"

Father's eyes are deep brown lakes of love. He is silent for a very long time. "You."

"Me, Father? What for? What can I do?"

"You can help them."

"But how, Father? How? I have no power. I have no money."

"Easy, darling," Father says in a calming voice. "I promise on your birthday you will understand."

Ride a cockhorse to Banbury Cross,
To see a fine lady upon a white horse;
Rings on her fingers and bells on her toes,
She shall have music wherever she goes.

CHAPTER 19

Dancing in the Woods

Now Father's words perplex me as much as Mother's, but he asked for rest as he felt tired and I obeyed his request. "Go to the dance and enjoy yourself," he said.

"You know of the dancing circle in the woods," I said.

"Know it?" Father laughed. "I believe your mother started it."

Lu, Nuff, and I at Nuff's house to pretty ourselves. Lu's father nearly forbade her to go out this evening, so angry was he at hearing about those royal boys bathing bare back. We have Tattlebug to thank for that. She heard Lu and me gigging about it when we met to share our noonday meal and then tattled the story to Lu's brother Dunder when he came to deliver the goat cheese Nora had ordered. Dunder, doof that he is, told Lu's father, embellishing the story a bit, saying that Lu and Nuff and I had joined the boys for a swim. Anyway . . . Nuff's good mother went to Lu's father to set the story straight, and finally he came to his senses. Good thing. Lu looks so very lovely tonight. Hopefully Sir Richard will be enchanted.

◇◇◇◇◇

The young people of Miramore have gathered to dance in the woods for as long as anyone can recall. Several yards into the thickest part of the forest there is suddenly a large open field where the land is flat and encircled by trees, Nature having obligingly created the perfect secluded dance floor. The first boys to arrive will light a fire in the rock pit in the center and those with pipes and fiddles and drums will claim spots on the bordering tree-stump seats to perform.

I look forward to these evenings, because I will get to dance. Dance, dance, dance, dance, dance, dance, dance! I would dance all night long if I could. I would dance until every star fell aslumber, until the sun nudged the moon from the sky.

But, of course, like my friends, I have a curfew.

◇◇◇◇◇

We take turns washing each other's hair using the sweetly scented chamomile and coconut shampoo Nuff's mother makes. Her soaps and oils, lotions, powders and lip-color sticks bring many a customer to her stall on Trading Day.

We towel dry our hair by the fire. Nuff hums a tune we know we'll hear tonight and soon Lu and I join in. So many a time such as this we've shared. I look from one friend's face to another. How very much I will miss them.

"Well," Lu says, braiding a thin white ribbon through her shining red hair, "you know I hope Sir Richard will find his way to the forest tonight, but after seeing Sir Marcus of Maple the other day, I wouldn't mind a dance with him."

"Trusting he found his clothes," Nuff whispers, and we burst out laughing, then hush as Nuff's mother's comes with some blush powder for our cheeks and a dab each of her new ginger-almond perfume.

"What are you girls laughing about now?" she says, shaking her head, smiling. "You're always laughing, laughing, laughing."

"Better that than the opposite," Nuff says.

"That's so," her mother says. "Take laughter over tears any day."

◇◇◇◇◇

Arms linked we head to the woods. I am wearing a pretty white dress and the emerald green shawl Father says matches my eyes, the oyster shell necklace from Mother about my neck.

The toad frogs and crickets' cacophony and the far-off strains of laughter are a prelude of the evening's music to come. The path is hard to see in the dark. We step carefully over gnarled tree roots and the occasional snake and rabbit hole, at last arriving safely to the clearing. Torches have been lit and the fire pit flames soar high. A full moon basks us in a light so bright he rivals his sister, sun.

We approach the gathering and greet our other friends from the island, steering clear of Tattlebug attempting to tag along behind us. All the Miramore boys our age are here, except Mackree. Where is Mackree?

"Oooh, look," Lu says. "The princes."

Sir Richard and Sir Peter, ever a pair, lead the pack. The Muffets nearly trip over each other rushing toward these two, most handsome of the PITs. Sir Richard wears a simple white shirt and black trousers. Sir Peter's hair hangs long about his shoulders, the silver hoop glinting in the firelight. I *am* lucky to have earned their sincere affection.

"Will you look at them," Lu says.

"*Hmmm-hmm*," Nuff answers.

The first strain of a fiddle breaks the night air.

"Shall we dance?" I say.

"Let's walk over near the PITs," Lu suggests.

A second and third fiddle join the first and my feet begin to move. "You two go, I'll catch up in a minute."

Never needing a partner when the music calls, I enter the circle, a smile lighting my face. The reel is fast and happy and I step fast and then faster with the rhythm, clapping my hands in the air, two-three. The tempo speeds up and I whirl and swirl free as a seagull in the wind. I see Sir Richard and Sir Peter walking toward me. My heart is pounding. I am giggling with joy, not because of the handsome princes, but because I am dancing. Dancing, dancing, dancing.

Feet stamping the ground, in and around the tree-stump musicians I dance, head moving to the beat, body swaying to the sound, hands clapping in measure, I hitch my skirt up so as not to stumble, feet step-stepping, circling, circling, my face aglow in the bonfire flames.

Dance to the fiddlers,
Dance to the fiddlers,
Dance to the fiddlers, whee!

The old rhyme plays in my mind as I dance, swishing and swirling and stepping and twirling, head thrown back, laughing with delight. Drums and flutes and tin whistles have joined the fiddles now, but it is the fiddle that I have always loved best.

"Cease, at once!" A voice slices the air. The music stops. I come to a dizzy halt.

"Dancing wild, unescorted, like some jezebel." It is Professor Pillage, the military arts instructor. He takes my arm and pulls me to the side. "You will cease this heathen display this instant. How shameful in the presence of our royal guests."

My heart is pounding from the dancing, and my

face reddens with embarrassment and then rage. I hear the Muffets sound their pleasure over my predicament. "Finally got her comeuppance," one says.

"Unarm the lady," Sir Peter says, coming forward in a most chivalrous manner.

"This instant," Sir Richard demands. "Are you all right, Lady Grace?" he says.

Professor Pillage salutes Sir Richard and steps back looking bewildered but obedient.

A fiddle takes up again and another joins in, this time in a slower beat. And then I see Mackree, leaning on a tree, arms folded, taking all of this in. *Why didn't he come to my defense?* I stood up for him without thinking when Sir Humbert disrespected him. Not that I needed rescuing. I am perfectly capable of defending myself from fools such as Pillage, but look how Sir Richard and Sir Peter reacted. Shouldn't Mackree, of all people, have been the first at my side? Even as I think this, though, I know I am being unfair. Mackree has set me free for another so that I may answer my call. Mackree has taken the harder, more noble route. Why can't I let him be? Almost as if he hears my thoughts, Mackree turns his back on me.

The music turns slower. "May I have this dance, pretty lady?" Sir Peter asks. Sir Richard backs away, ever chivalrous, but pats his heart as if to say, *Me next?*

Mackree is still standing there. But then he is gone,

and I find myself nodding to Sir Richard in spite of myself.

"Lady Grace?" Sir Peter says.

"Thank you." I curtsy, smile, and take his outstretched hand.

And so I dance a second time with the handsome pirate prince of Elmland. I feel someone staring at me. I look, assuming it is Tattlebug.

No, it is Nuff. She smiles encouragingly at me, and I try my best to smile back.

Jack and Jill went up the hill
To fetch a pail of water;
Jack fell down and broke his crown,
And Jill came tumbling after.

CHAPTER 20

The Whale

Next morning I walk to the beach with a vengeance, still smarting from Mackree's slight. I mount the bluff and there he is. Sitting on a rock, staring out at the water. I walk quickly to him. He looks up, his beautiful thick brown hair a curtain over his eyes. He flicks his hair from his forehead to see me. "Mornin', Pearl," he says.

"*Mornin', Pearl?* Is that all you have to say to me? Mornin' Pearl?"

"I'm sorry I don't talk like your fancy princes, *etcetera*," he says. "Which one are ya choosin' anyway?" He throws a rock and then another. "I hear one's courtin' ya with pink roses and the other with red, out strollin' the beach at night with one, dancing with the other . . ."

Tattlebug, that troublemaker. I ought to give her something to sneeze about.

Mackree stands up to walk away.

"Mackree, wait," I whisper, reaching out to touch his back.

He swings around brusquely, takes me in his arms, and kisses me.

Mackree is kissing me. Then I am kissing him. Oh, please heavens, make this moment never end.

He pulls away from me and turns to leave. I'm so startled I nearly tumble off the rock. "Mackree, please . . ."

A spout of water sprays straight up out of the sea and we both look.

"A whale," I say.

"Yes," Mackree says. He stays next to me.

We watch as the sleek black tail of the sea-giant, splayed into perfectly curved equal halves, rises dramatically into the air, then sinks softly back into the azure sea, with nary a telltale ripple.

I move closer to Mackree, breathing in the smell of the soap he uses to scrub his horses. "Stay with me," I ask.

I sit on the boulder and he sits beside me. We stare out at the waves in silence.

There is something about a whale that demands your attention. Mackree and I sit soundlessly, no words necessary, allowing ourselves to forget our circumstance in this perfect moment. Our eyes search the water east and west, waiting hopefully as so many other human beings have done all through time, hoping one of these mesmerizing graceful giants will breach for us again.

It doesn't reappear. Most likely leagues away from Miramore now, treating who knows next to its ancient magical sea ballet.

I steal a quick look at Mackree's beautiful face. My heart swells. But, no. No, no, no, no, no. "I saw Nuff visiting with your mother," I say. "Nuff is the greatest catch on the island, for sure. She's smart and pretty and she loves Miramore as much as you do. If I can't . . ." My voice cracks.

"Stop," Mackree says, his face a confusing jumble of emotion.

He puts something in my palm and closes my hand over it like a shell.

I open my hand. It's a rock. Smooth and black. "Shaped like a whale," I say with a little laugh.

"Found it on the beach this morning, just before you came," Mackree says, his eyes searching mine.

"A sign," I say.

"Maybe," he says, shrugging his shoulders, "or just a good skipping stone."

Before I can speak, he is gone.

Four and twenty tailors went to kill a snail,
The best man among them durst not touch her tail.
She put out her horns like a little Kyloe cow,
Run, tailors, run, or she'll kill you e'en now.

CHAPTER 21

Field Trips

Professor Millington soon announces she is taking the royals on her annual week-long field trip into the forest to help them get in touch with their "inner yins." The princes groan in unison.

From our listening post beneath the classroom window, Nuff, Lu, and I cover our mouths to silence the giggles.

"Remember the year she had them weave flowers through their hair and skip through the meadow," Lu whispers.

"And don't forget the daisies," I say. Professor Millington always teaches the princes the "loves me, loves me not," plucking game.

"Each of us," Professor Millington is saying "has a female and male, a yin and yang nature. Despite what you young men may have been told about bravery and bravado, I assure you that a young lady finds it particularly charming when a boy she likes casts aside aggressive, competitive tendencies to show his more sensitive and vulnerable side . . . to let down the iron shackles and lay bare the contents of his heart. And tears, my young men"—she sighs—"tears are very, very good. Tears are icing on the cake."

The PITs groan. "Trying to turn us into snivelers, are you?" Sir Humpty says.

I picture the princes sitting around a campfire, roasting marshmallows, sharing deep secrets until they're all bawling like babes in the nursery.

"A floppy bunch of emotes," Sir Marcus says.

"What's an emote?" Lu whispers

"An emotional person?" Nuff suggests.

"Like the three of us," I say, sighing with a smile.

⬦⬦⬦⬦⬦

When the PITs return from bonding with their "inner yins," Professor Pillage is ready and waiting with a field trip plan of his own. He instructs the royal students to pack up for a week of "real man" sports—archery and trapping and hunting. He orders Mackree to prepare the horses. He calls for some hounds. Lady Jule is not pleased, but as with the race at the tournament, she knows she must follow the bidding of an emissary of the Order.

I send a silent prayer to the forest animals: *Run, quick, and hide.*

Killing animals for food may be Nature's way. Killing animals for sport is wrong.

❖❖❖❖❖

August has brought a western breeze to Miramore, and a blistering heat as well. Father's health is returning, but under Doctor's orders he is to stay home and rest, no work until further notice. Healthy food and rest are the prescription.

I can tell Father misses running the kitchen. Summer is his shining season. And I know that as he sips the clear vegetable soup Nurse Hartling brings to him and the fruit salads Lady Jule sends, he dreams of succulent roasts and pot pies and freshly baked bread, butter melting.

I decide to take a field trip of my own.

As much as I enjoy the company of Lu and Nuff, I am just as happy, maybe even happier, when I am alone.

"Sometimes your best company is you," Mother says inside, and I smile.

I change into my swimming clothes, pack some food and a jug of water, and head toward the sea. It is a sunny, glorious day. Throwing my sandals and towel on the sand, I run and dive straight into the water, sweeping my arms like a butterfly, kicking my long strong legs out like a frog. I surface and fill my lungs to the full and dive again, deeper this time. I reach out to touch the yellow tang and then a blue striped starling. A giant sea turtle moves silently past me and I watch as it pecks delicately at the rough coral, sending bits of pink snow to coat the mermen's shaving brushes sticking up from the ocean floor.

It is an entire other world under here, every bit as beautiful as the one above. The grandfather turtle's murky eye meets mine and I think of Professor Pillage and the hounds and the hunt. Be safe, my furry and featured friends. You know the forest better than he. *Hide.*

Back on the beach, I dry off and lie back on my towel. I close my eyes. Soon I am dreaming.

I am standing alone up high in a tower looking down. A multitude of faces are gazing up at me. I am speaking. What am I saying? The people are listening. What am I saying? Suddenly the people are smiling, their hands clasped jubilantly in the air.

I wake feeling excited. This is a new dream, one that breeds hope in my heart. Perhaps there can be joy without Mackree. I slip my skirt and blouse over my now dry bathing clothes and walk the beach hoping for words of wisdom from Mother, but she is surprisingly silent.

I look for signs, but it seems each thing that calls to me, upon examination, is just one of the thin, flat stones Mackree once loved to skip. Out of habit, I pick them up.

One, two, three. It seems all today's signs are pointing one way. I gather more and more skipping stones. I find myself needing to see him desperately. But I will not break my silent promise to myself or to him, and so the weight of the foolish stones hangs heavy in my pockets, nearly as heavy as my heart.

Baa, baa, black sheep
Have you any wool?
Yes, sir, yes, sir,
Three bags full:
One for my master,
And one for my dame,
And one for the little boy,
Who lives down the lane.
Baa, baa, black sheep,
Have you any wool?
Yes, sir, yes, sir,
Three bags full.

CHAPTER 22

The Sabbath

I peel an orange and make a pot of tea. I open the sack of
sweet pastries Nora Baker brought yesterday along with
the fresh roasted turkey, conch chowder, and corn.

"The sweets are fer you," she said. "Don't be feeding
them to Cook. He's gotta watch his diet."

That was nice of Nora. I bit into a fig muffin.
"Mmmm . . . Delicious."

"Just day-old stuff I'd be tossin' anyway," the old

woman had said, but I could tell it was more than that.

I stuff two rolls in my pocket for the cats and head to the beach for my walk. No need to rush this morning. It is the Sabbath, the day of rest and renewal and gratitude.

Monday's child is fair of face,
Tuesday's child is full of grace,

The rhyme rings in my head as I walk. I was born on Tuesday.

Wednesday's child is full of woe,
Thursday's child has far to go,
Friday's child is loving and giving,
Saturday's child has to work for a living,
But a child that's born on the Sabbath day,
Is fair and wise and good and gay.

What day of the week was Mackree born on? Why don't I know that? Not that it matters. I must put him out of my head . . .

When I reach the water, the sky is shrouded dark with clouds, and the foamy white caps on the waves let me know a storm is brewing. A breeze swirls toward me, throwing stinging sand up against my legs. I see Captain Jessie at the docks covering up his boat. I wave to him and he waves back. Such an odd goose he is. I don't see him mixing with the royals or the men of Miramore either.

The beach is strewn with clumps of black-green seaweed. I stoop to pick up a small yellow heart-shaped rock. There is a tiny white pebble, it almost looks like a pearl, imbedded in the middle. I try to dislodge it with my fingernail, but as hard as I try, the pearl won't budge.

Overhead, a sleek black duck screeches by, and then a second one flaps up behind it. Side by side now, they fly off together. I stop and watch the pair until they are but small black dots disappearing into the veil of fog.

The wind whips my hair out behind me. A powerful gust sweeps gritty sand up into my face. I wipe the stinging specks from my eyes and gathering my collar tighter around my neck, I set off for home, my heart-shaped sea-sign to ponder.

As it is Sunday, I do not have to scoop coal or pick vegetables or toil in the kitchen under Nora's command. The bells of the chapel pierce the quiet morning air and I nod and smile hello to friends and neighbors as they walk toward the carved wooden entrance door, the smell of incense and the sound of music intensifying in the village air each time the heavy door is opened. One of the Muffets, Clarissa Porter, passes by me with her family, raising her nose as if she is better, superior to me.

When I reach home I am surprised to see Father leaving the cottage with Nurse Hartling, who is donned in a pretty blue dress and a straw hat with a flowered scarf. "Time the patient gets some exercise," she says to me as they pass.

Father winks at me and shrugs his shoulders.

"Following Doctor's orders," he says. He extends his arm to Nurse Hartling and I swear she blushes as she accepts it.

Well, I'll be. I smile. Lady Jule has serious competition. She'd better bring more sweets tout de suite.

Inside the cottage, I busy myself filling up the straw baskets. Each Sunday I bring them to villagers who might need cheering up. Mother started the Sabbath tradition and I continue it still.

Lining each basket with a cloth napkin, I put in some of Nora's baked treats, and a few pretty shells, fresh sprigs of flowers from the garden. Nothing fancy. "Your presence, not the presents," is what Mother says matters.

First to Sister Varley, my kindergarten teacher, ninety-something now and slow-moving from arthritis, but her mind is still sharp as a sword. I make us some tea and she sets up the checkers. "I've looked forward to your visit all week," she says.

Next to our neighbor Rowena, bed-bound with the flu. I tell her funny news about the PITs and about the whale Mackree and I saw spouting.

"You've brightened my day, Gracepearl," she says.

I look up the path toward Mackree's house. Nuff is coming down it. My heart clenches. When she reaches me she says she's sorry but she must hurry home. Her mother is expecting her.

When I have delivered the last basket, I head back home. Nurse Hartling has gone and Father is reading.

"Oh good, daughter, come," he says, motioning to me to sit beside him. "We had another visitor while you were gone."

"Another lady calling on my handsome father?" I say, teasing.

"No, as a matter of fact. It was a suitor for you."

The first name in my mind is Mackree.

"One of the princes, a most impressive young man."

I cannot hide my disappointment, though this is what I have wanted. "Who?"

"He asked my blessing before he asks you for your hand in marriage."

"Which one, Father?" Pray let it be Peter.

"You mean there could be more than one?" Father says, grinning.

"Stop teasing me, Father." I push his arm gently, so he knows that I am serious. "Name him."

Father laughs heartily. He clutches his fist to his chest, a flash of pain crossing his face. "I am not teasing you, Gracepearl," he says, smiling. "Although you indeed have many virtues, daughter, patience is not among them. The prince asked that his identity be kept secret so that he may profess his intentions to you at the ball."

"Oh, Father, just a hint then?"

Father laughs again. "Let me suffice to say, daughter,

that I found this young man to be a most decent human being of the noblest sort who clearly has your best interests in mind, and after conversing with him at length, I said that if your heart's desire matched his, then who am I to stand betwixt a couple and Cupid's arrow. And with that, I gave him my blessing. The decision, of course, is yours, Gracepearl. Yours and yours alone."

Curlylocks, Curlylocks,
Wilt thou be mine?
Thou shalt not wash dishes
Nor yet feed the swine,
But sit on a cushion
And sew a fine seam,
And feed upon strawberries,
Sugar and cream.

CHAPTER 23

Proposals

In the days that follow, I am befuddled trying to figure out whether Sir Richard or Sir Peter asked for my hand in marriage. The old Gracepearl would have run in an instant to tell Nuff and Lu, but yet I feel called to keep this matter to myself for the moment. I am fairly certain Tattlebug has kept them informed of all my dates this summer, but they are so sweet they have not said a word. I fear hurting them, and I fear hurting myself. I need time to hear the contents of my own heart.

I trip and send a pail full of coal nuggets tumbling

down the hill. I walk all the way to the garden forgetting Nora's list. I pick a peck of yellow peppers when Nora clearly specified green. "Where is your brain, girl," the old wrinkled cook scolded. "I wrote it there, plain as day, see." She pointed to the list.

I look, yes, there it was, plain as day. "Greene."

Which prince spoke with Father? The memory of Sir Humpty leering at me in the garden at the start of summer slinks into my mind. I cringe. That egg prince stares at me every chance he gets. Last week Tattlebug said he tried to get information about me from her once he learned we worked together in the kitchen.

"He's really very nice," Tattlebug said with a dreamy look in her eyes. Does Tattlebug fancy Sir Humpty? *Eeew.* Well, at least she is finally over Mackree, even if Nuff . . . I stop this thought, but where my mind goes is no more helpful. Sir Richard? Sir Peter?

I see Mackree's face. The pull is strong as a tidal wave, and yet it cannot be . . . Oh, please, Mother, give me some direction. I am so confused.

✧✧✧✧✧

At lunch in the shade of the trees, Lu and Nuff sense my conflicted and jittery mood. Have they heard tattle of a proposal awaiting me at the ball? But they do not pry, do not judge, and our silence is full of friendship.

"Professor Robinson gave a lecture on grooming

today," Lu reports. "I was hoping he'd speak on the art of chamber pot archery, but he focused on ear wax and foot fungus."

"Eeew, I've lost my appetite," I say.

Nuff laughs and claps. "More, more."

Lu shares a bit about the techniques of nose-hair plucking.

Nuff tells how the Muffets are sewing elaborately ornamented banners with the home crest of their favorite PIT for tomorrow's tournament.

I smile but find myself bored with the conversation. The tournament and then my birthday, soon after, the Summersleave Ball. Then September and the royal ships return. A prince is my only passage from here. Which one wants to marry me?

When I get home Father is propped up in bed with a box of ribbon candy. "Someone came calling," he says.

"Lady Jule?" I say. "Nurse Hartling would not approve. Father, I fear I must chaperone you."

Father laughs a hearty belly laugh that ends in a cough. "No," he says. "It was another prince, seeking my daughter's hand."

What? Just when it seems I cannot be more dizzy, the world swirls crazier.

Here, at last, must be Mother's choice. A choice between two princes, two safe passages from the island to answer the call beyond. That notion seemed so light and whimsical back when the ships first landed. Now the thought weighs me down like an anchor.

Two princes. Fine men indeed. But neither is the prince of my heart.

Shoe the horse, shoe the mare,
But let the little colt go bare.

CHAPTER 24

The Tournament

The annual summer tournament is a much anticipated holiday on Miramore, and this year more than ever, I note. Work ceases mid-morning so that we can gather to watch. There is only one stand for spectators, and that, of course, is for the professors. Pillage observes the scene smugly, like a rooster proudly surveying his fighting flock. Lady Jule fidgets and chews honey drops with an anxious line set in her brow. I see Captain Jessie sitting by himself. I wonder what he's been up to.

Lu and Nuff and I lay a quilted blanket on the hill, a good place for viewing but not the best. The Muffets claimed the best spot, probably at dawn. Dressed in their matching pink shawls, hair all curled and ribboned, they sit on cushions under umbrellas, holding banners for their favorite princes.

The majority of the banners, I note, are for Ashland

and Elm, Clarissa and Sally hold flags for Maple, Janey for Hickory. None for Oak, I note with satisfaction.

Just then Tattlebug, wearing a dress way too small for her and shoes so big she is tottering, comes looking for a spot to sit. She is carrying a ragged banner with a painted-on leaf of oak, the emblem of Sir Humpty Dumpty.

"Even the egg prince has a fan," Lu says.

How brave of Tattlebug, I think.

One of the Muffets, Sally Tailor, shouts out something to the stumbling girl, most likely a taunt, and the other Muffets laugh. And despite all Tattlebug has done to annoy me, I feel bad for her in this moment.

Tattlebug pulls at the skirt of her dress as if to make it longer. She lowers her head and the banner. She raises her hand to her nose, no doubt for a sneeze, slips out of her shoe, and falters to a fall, to more gales of Muffet laughter, then ducks in with a group of children, slinking to a seat behind Leem and Brine.

I am going to do something kind for Tattlebug. Next Sunday, a basket for sure.

The Muffets gasp as Sir Richard appears, mounted on Mackree's prize steed. Thank goodness Ransom wasn't wasted on the likes of Humpty Dumpty.

The Muffets toss flowers on the path as Sir Richard approaches. He smiles but doesn't acknowledge them. When he passes by me and Nuff and Lu, he slows down to a cantor and graciously nods his head in a sweep that takes in all three of us.

We curtsy.

"Did you see that," Lu gushes. "He smiled right at me."

I feel a pang of disloyalty. What if Lu hears of Sir Richard's intentions toward me, before I have a chance to tell her? She would think me a poor friend, a traitor indeed. I vow to speak with Lu right after the last event.

Sir Peter is next to process before the stands. The Muffets toss daisies before him. Sir Peter catches one, pats his heart and waves, sending squeals of delight up from the pink-shawled chorus. When the pirate prince reaches the three of us, he nods his head very gentleman-like, then kisses the daisy and sends it flying toward us.

Nuff catches it. "He's a devil, that one," she says in a voice that is barely a whisper.

"So you fancy him, Nuff," I blurt out.

There. Now at least I'll know for sure.

"What's not to fancy?" she says.

"But are you serious about him?" I ask.

"It doesn't matter," she says. She looks at me. "He is serious about another."

"What do you mean, Nuff?" I demand.

"Sir Peter is your portal," Nuff says. "Please, Grace, don't make this so hard."

Her harsh voice protects her emotions from escaping.

"Your dream is to leave. He has the ship you need. Return his advances and be done with it . . ."

"But when I saw you at Mackree's—"

"Not now, Grace," Nuff pleads.

"Look girls, Sir Humpty," Lu squeals, and we turn our attention back to the field. The egg prince is wearing a most audacious ermine-trimmed coat. I see Tattlebug waving her banner with a flourish, but Humpty doesn't take note.

Now Sir Marcus of Maple struts onto the field, then Sir Blake of Birch . . . until finally the last of the PITs process by.

Today there will be six events in the tournament, beginning with Pillage's race. At the end, the prince with the most points will have his named inscribed on the wall of honor in the banquet hall. The House of Ash and the House of Elm have the greatest number of winners. I counted the other day. The princes have been teasing Sir Humpty, as there has never been a victor from the House of Oak.

"You wait and see," he boasted at dinner the other night. "This will be the year of the Oak."

My heart skips a beat when I see Mackree, his long shaggy bangs covering his eyes like a drapery. He motions and calls orders to his brothers and the other stable hands, and they work to get the horses into their starting positions.

I can feel the professors' tension and the Muffets' excitement in the air.

The horn blows and: "They're off!"

The contestants will circle the field three times. Sir Peter takes the lead from the start, his black ponytail whipping out behind him. Sir Richard is close on his heels. Sir Marcus of the birthday suit is third. Humpty Dumpty's horse is last. Flaming mad, he barks something at Mackree when he passes the first turn.

Whips and rods are now allowed in the tournament, and Sir Humpty doesn't seem to know any other way to win a race. Thank goodness it is not Ransom he lashes today.

The horses gallop faster, several neck to neck as they start the second loop. And as exciting as the race is, the crowd cheering, the Muffets screeching, most eyes on Sir Richard as he now masterfully claims the field, I find myself looking only at Mackree. His eyes glued to his beloved Ransom racing a prince on a field of glory, willing his horse to win even, I imagine, as he detests the violence of the new rules for all his dear horses.

And then Mackree's hands are on his hair, sweeping it away in a most violent way and I see the look of horror on his face, a loud whinnying, groans and gasps all around me, and I swing to follow Mackree's gaze.

Sir Richard is on the ground. Mackree races to him. Sir Peter has pulled up on his own steed to turn around.

The other riders have not noticed, they continue at a breakneck speed. Sir Humbert beats his heels mercilessly into his horse's sweating flanks. He reaches into the preposterously big coat and pulls out a whipping rod and strikes his old gray horse. He strikes and strikes and strikes the horse again. Mackree is helping Sir Richard limp off the field. Professor Pillage motions Mackree away. Mackree turns, no doubt to see to Ransom, and in that instant he's knocked down and trampled beneath the hind hooves of Sir Humbert's whip-crazed horse.

Little Miss Muffet
Sat on a tuffet,
Eating some curds and whey.
Along came a spider,
And sat down beside her,
And frightened Miss Muffet away.

CHAPTER 25

Princes Before Peasants

Although he is yards away, I am the first to reach Mackree.

His eyes are closed, blood oozing from an awful gash on his forehead.

"Mackree." I slide my hands gently beneath his head, lowering my cheek to his nose to feel if he is breathing.

Thank goodness, he is.

There are loud frantic calls for assistance as Professor Pillage and others tend to Sir Richard across the way. Lady Jule has fainted.

"The doctor! A stretcher! A blanket!" Pillage shouts.

People scurry to do his bidding. Doctor Jeffers is coming from the stands.

Mackree's younger brother Mick is standing there watching me. "You oughtn't move him, Gracepearl, case his neck is broke."

"Get Nurse Hartling from the hospital *now*," I shout. "Run!"

I rest Mackree's head on my lap. He doesn't make a sound. I refuse to cry. My heart pounds as if it will burst. I pull the scarf from my neck and press it against the wound on his forehead, hoping to staunch the bleeding.

"Mackree, my heart." I speak loudly in his ear, strong and confident. "Help comes. Hold on."

I stroke his forehead. I kiss his closed eyelids. My blood freezes and boils, freezes and boils. I feel I will explode. In this moment, the power of truth overwhelms me. Here in my arms is the love of my life. My feelings for Mackree have grown as I have grown. We are no longer children. He was right. The days of sand castles and skipping stones are over. I don't just love Mackree Byre, I am *in love* with him. Why aren't people coming to help? I kiss his hair, his cheeks, his eyelashes. "I love you. I love you. I love you. I love you."

Nuff and Lu reach me now. I feel their hands lightly touching my shoulders, one on each side. "What can we do?" Nuff says.

"I've sent for Nurse Hartling," I say. "Pray."

Over there, the Muffets are swarming about the

makeshift bed that's been set up for Sir Richard. Doctor Jeffers is attending him and the professors are hovering near. The Muffets are whimpering into their handkerchiefs. Doesn't anyone care about Mackree!

Tattlebug kneels beside me. She holds out a tin cup. "Some water?" she says.

"Thank you," I say, grateful for the kindness. I bring the cup to Mackree's lips and try to give him a sip, but the water dribbles down his chin.

There is a commotion on the field nearby. "You snarling yellow-bellied . . ." Sir Peter is shouting, yanking Sir Humbert by his lace-trimmed collar. "I saw you beat that horse, you dog. If you killed my friend, I'll kill you!" Sir Peter punches Sir Humpty so hard surely his shell will crack.

Where is Nurse Hartling? "Stay with me, Mackree," I say, not a wish, a command.

After a while, Doctor Jeffers stands and moves out into a clearing. "Sir Richard will be fine," he pronounces. The assembled crowd cheers. Professor Pillage nearly weeps with relief. I nearly vomit with disgust and worry.

Nuff runs to the doctor and pleads with him to come attend to Mackree now that the prince is okay.

"Princes before peasants," Tattlebug says to me, shaking her head angrily, "always been so, always will be." She sneers at some Muffets who have come to hover

over us in search of new drama now that Sir Richard is off to the hospital.

"Get away, ya spiders," she says, thrusting out her hands to swat them off.

"That's right. Go!" Nuff says to the Muffets. She and Lu spread their arms out around Mackree and me.

"Leave them be," Lu says.

I close my eyes. A child is there in my mind. With sunken eyes and hollowed cheeks. "Please," she says, "I am starving."

The lion and the unicorn
Were fighting for the crown;
The lion beat the unicorn
All about the town.
Some gave them white bread,
And some gave them brown;
Some gave them plum cake,
And sent them out of town.

CHAPTER 26

Nobility

Mackree lives! Thank the heavens, gods and goddesses, goodness, everything.

The wound on his forehead was deep, but it will heal. He heard me crying out to him as he lay injured on the field, but he pretended not to hear. This he confessed to me when his family had left the hospital room and I lingered longer.

"I wanted to be sure ya loved me," he explained.

"*What?*" I said. "I was scared near to death for you!"

"Aye," he says with a weak smile. "'Twas a mean trick, Pearl. I am sorry."

"You know how I feel about you," I say.

"Aye," he says, "and I wanted to feel it one last time before you go."

"But I—"

"Tattlebug suspects you'll be getting two offers at the ball."

"Mackree . . ." My head is throbbing. I look at his bloodied lip. I want to kiss those lips. "I wasn't ready before, but now my feelings for you are different. I will not leave you."

"Pearl, I see how you are called from Miramore. Your path is clear. Choose a prince and go."

"No, Mackree." I touch his hair. He flinches.

I lean in toward him. He turns away.

"Go, Pearl, now."

I shake my head, crying. "No." Even as I know he is right.

"All I ever wanted was you, Pearl. You want me and something more. Something I can never give you. I may not be a prince, but I can't be a man either and know I've denied you your dreams."

"Mackree."

"Please, Pearl, go. Have courage. *Go.*"

I rush from the hospital, feeling cleaved in half, bewildered, beheaded, bleeding. How can life be so cruel? Destiny draws me, the call is so fierce, every fiber of my being, like a tide pull not denied. I am willing to accept. To set course for the unknown. But must I leave my heart to dry up dead as fish, as driftwood on the hot, parched Miramore sand?

How noble of Mackree to set me free. To insist I heed this call. He is as much a prince as Richard or Peter or any of them.

Cruel, cruel fate.

❖ ❖ ❖ ❖ ❖

A week passes. Mackree and Sir Richard are both discharged from the hospital and are up and around again.

Today is August 10, the morning of my sixteenth birthday.

I walk to the beach before dawn, climb the steps to the top of the old bell tower. I watch the sky blush pink and then orange, then close my eyes from the blinding light as the sun births a brilliant new day.

Happy birthday, dearest daughter, Mother's voice sings sweet inside me. *Happy birthday to you, happy birthday to you, happy birthday, dear . . .*

"Mother. I am frightened."

I open my eyes and look down at the water. The tide crashes in upon the rocks. I step back scared from the opening, pull my cloak about me.

Fear is a pebble, Pearl, a grain of sand. Should you choose to accept this day's gift, you will have power as great as the sea within you. It is already there, daughter. It has always been. You alone can claim it.

"Gracepearl! Gracepearl!"

I look down at the beach.

Tattlebug.

"Come to the hospital," she screams up to me. "Hurry!"

Oh no. I nearly stumble racing down the stairs.

"It's Cook," Tattlebug says, all out of breath when I reach her. "It's bad I fear, Grace, run. I'll go fetch Mackree fer ya."

❖ ❖ ❖ ❖ ❖

"I'm sorry, dear," Nurse Hartling says, tears welling in her eyes when she sees me in the hallway. "He asks for you. Go to him."

No. I rush to the now familiar room. Father's eyes are closed, but I see his hefty belly rising up and down with air. I rest my head on his chest. *Be strong,* I shout a silent command to Father's heart. *Don't fail Father now. Do you hear me!*

Someone comes into the room. I turn.

Mackree. He comes to my side. "Pearl," he says, awkwardly. "Happy birthday."

I feel my heart slice in two.

Father opens his eyes. He smiles at me. He nods a warm welcome to Mackree. "Do me a favor, son?"

"Anything, sir," Mackree says with great earnest.

Father reaches to his neck. With effort he raises his head and lifts the thin leather rope with the key up and over. He instructs Mackree to bring the trunk from beneath his bed in the cottage. "Posthaste, son. Run."

"I shall return in an instant," Mackree says, and dashes off.

I kneel beside my father, trying to force a cheerful, confident smile, but I was never good at masking true emotions.

"My dearest daughter," Cook says in a labored voice, no longer veiling the pain weighing heavy on his chest. "I am not long for this world."

"Father!" I wail. "Please, stay. You cannot leave me. You must not leave me. You are the only family I have."

Father smiles, lifting a shaking hand to stroke my hair. "Soon I will join my beloved Miriam, but please do not despair. Just has your mother has never left you for a moment, I promise you, neither shall I."

Lucy Locket lost her pocket,
Kitty Fisher found it;
There was not a penny in it,
But a ribbon round it.

CHAPTER 27

A Revelation

Mackree is back, the fastest runner on Miramore, carrying the purple trunk.

"Set it here, son," Father says, patting the space beside him.

My heart clenches at his use of the name "son." It might have been. Once in another life, another time, it might have been. I turn away to wipe the tears from my eyes. I must have courage for Father.

He unlocks the trunk. I stand back by Mackree.

"This year there will be three gifts," Father says.

"No, Father, just the sixteenth . . . *please*. Keep the seventeenth for next year, and the eighteenth for the year after that."

Mackree squeezes my arm as if to strengthen me.

"Please, daughter," Father says in a halting voice, "there may not be much time."

I stop trying to stop the inevitable. I lean my head on Mackree's shoulder.

Father fumbles in the trunk. He pulls out a book.

"Go ahead," he says, "open it."

I take the leather volume from his hands. It is the book of history Mother used to teach me from. I turn back the cover. Father has written something there. I'd recognize his handwriting anywhere.

"'To our beloved daughter, Gracepearl, on the occasion of her sixteenth birthday.'"

There is a sheaf of papers stuck inside the back cover. I turn to them, again recognizing Father's cursive scrawl.

This must have been what he was writing that day in the cottage.

"Read it," Father says.

I pick up the papers and begin. "Once upon a time . . ." My voice shakes as I read. And then I hear Mother's voice reading the story aloud to me as my eyes follow the words.

Once upon a time there was a princess who, as she stood with her mother and father in the tower waving down to the subjects gathered to honor them each day, had begun to wonder why the people of the kingdom looked so sad. She asked her nurse, who bitterly explained that the people were hungry, sick, and homeless. Why then couldn't her parents help them? *"Your parents have tried to help, dear girl, but the forces against them are too powerful. It will take a mightier strength to turn the tides of this mass misfortune."*

The princess could not erase those faces from her mind. She vowed that if one day she took the throne, she would melt all the crowns, all the gold in the palace, and help the people who haunted her dreams.

At the mention of the dreams, I gasp and shudder.

Father nods at me. Mother reads on . . .

Mass rebellion broke out and war ensued. To protect their daughter, the princess's parents sent her off in the charge of a trusted sea captain. The captain delivered the princess and her baggage to an island enshrouded by a circle of mist, a place where royal families sent princes to study the charming arts in summer. It was winter and only the servants who lived on the island year-round were there. The sea captain left the princess in the safekeeping of a kitchen baker who, as fate would have it, was already providing safe haven for a young Pine duke also sent to escape the war.

Years passed and the young royals fell in love. She gathered fruits and vegetables, gave names to all the fish. He became quite a good cook. She loved to dance. He learned to play the fiddle.

My pulse pounds so I fear I may faint. I look at Father. His eyes are closed and he's smiling. Mother reads on . . .

When the time was right, they professed marriage vows in

the forest beneath a pine canopy, stars twinkling like diamonds above them. Years passed and the Royal Order, now but twelve branches, as the king and queen of Pine had been killed and there was no apparent heir, kept the summer school for princes in good operation. The Order feared the working-class ranks were growing disillusioned with the throne and more charm might provide a calming tonic. The people always liked a good show.

The island's royal couple, still keeping their lineage a secret, gave birth to a child, a daughter. And on that bright August day when she was born, they determined to raise her free of the burden of royal patronage and expectation. This girl would have a childhood full of the joys of nature, the sea, the forest, and the field. She would acquire humility forged from hard labor, compassion wrought from service to others, the friendship of those who would love her for the kindness of her character, not the cash in her coffers, and she would have peaceful stretches of solitude, so quiet she could hear the wisdom of her truth and one day choose her calling, whatever that would be.

My body is shaking. Mackree's hand supports my back.

I shut the book. Father's eyes search mine.

"Is it true?" I ask in a struggled whisper.

"Yes," Father says.

His face winces and he touches his chest. He reaches into the trunk and takes out a large envelope, wrapped in a purple ribbon with a gold seal. "Here are the papers to prove it, Gracepearl. Here is your seventeenth gift."

My head swoons. I sit down on the chair.

Father winces again. "You were to have two years to consider your decision, but with my health, now—"

"I'll get the doctor," Mackree says.

"Father," I shout, standing.

The pain subsides. His face softens. "It's gone," he says. "Stay, Mackree. Here, Gracepearl, the final gift."

Father reaches into the trunk. He takes out a purple satin box, tied with a gold ribbon.

There is an envelope, "Happy birthday, Gracepearl," in Mother's writing, on top.

I unseal the envelope and read the letter, again hearing Mother's voice inside.

My dearest daughter, Gracepearl, in whom we are so delighted.

Being your mother was the greatest joy of my life. I hope you have found pleasure in my birthday gifts to you through the years. With this last present, the trunk is empty, and yet, like your life, full of possibility.

Today you are an adult, my daughter, so you may choose to take your throne.

This moment is yours. You alone will write the next chapter.

It is for these reasons that I say to you, the gift inside this box may be destiny or decoration. It will be for you, and you alone to decide, our beautiful, precious, beloved daughter, Princess Gracepearl Cole.

I hear Mother laugh gently.

That is Cole with an "e." C . . . o . . . l . . . e.

With trembling hands, I untie the ribbon, open the box, and lift out the last gift.

A crown.

I am keeling, the room is reeling. Mackree wraps his arms about me.

I look at my father. "But, what now . . ."

"My darling," he says, "this is overwhelming news. Please forgive me if you think I should have told you sooner."

"No, Father. It isn't that. It's just, what do I do now? What does this all mean?"

"You can still take your time, Gracepearl," Father says. "Whether I live or die, you have a choice. It will be a shock to the branches, to the Order, to the world, that a sturdy sapling of the thirteenth branch, the noble House of Pine, lives on. In that envelope is all of the paperwork, the letters and documents you will need to claim the throne—in my absence, it can be yours before you turn eighteen."

My hand reaches out, then back, trembling.

"Or, burn the papers," Father says, "and keep the crown for whimsy when you dance in the woods."

My head is throbbing. I look at Mackree.

"Ahhh!" Father shouts, his face contorted in pain.

He struggles for air. Mackree rushes for help.

"Cook!" Nurse Hartling races in, then off to get the doctor.

"Father, *Father.*" I kiss his cheek, tears raining down on his beloved face.

"Happy birthday, darling daughter," he whispers. "Enjoy your gifts."

"The only gift I want is you," I sob. "You, Father."

"Sing me something, princess," he says.

I gulp and begin to sing a lullaby, one Mother often sang to me. The melody is light as a breeze, the words soft and warm as a blanket. My voices catches on the word in the lyric "ma-kree." *My heart.*

"I'm here, Pearl," Mackree says, holding me. I am here. Don't worry. I'm here."

Pussy cat, pussy cat,
where have you been?
I've been to London
to visit the Queen.
Pussy cat, pussy cat,
What did you there?
I frightened a little mouse
under the chair.

CHAPTER 28

Pearl's Place of Peace

Father still breathes, but just barely. He sleeps and sleeps and sleeps. I do not leave his side.

"He may never awaken," Doctor Jeffers says. "You must brace yourself for that."

"No," I say. "I won't."

Mackree stays with me as much as he can, but his duties call him to the stables each day. Lu and Nuff bring me food and company. "Go home and rest," Lu implores me. "We will stay," Nuff says. But I will not leave my father's side.

I pray to Mother to intercede on Father's behalf. "Please let him live, God, please."

Finally, on the fourth day, Nurse Hartling insists I go home for a rest. She will not take no for an answer. "You need fresh air, Gracepearl. Go now, go. I'll attend to him constantly, I assure you."

I walk home in a daze, like a ghost in a dream.

At the cottage, I boil water and bathe myself. I wash my hair and put on clean clothes. I pick up the jeweled mirror and look at my reflection.

There in the corner is the purple trunk Mackree carried back here from the hospital. The memory of the revelation sweeps over me, but all I can think about is Father.

"Mother, why are you so silent of late? Why do you not speak to me?"

I walk to Father's room, pick up the pine pillow and press it to my nose, breathing in the comforting scent, a soothing salve for my spirit.

My place of peace beckons. I hurry to the forest.

Passing by the kettle pond where Mackree and I first held hands, I pause and dip my hand into the water. It is soft and warm. I touch my fingers to my lips, remembering the kiss we shared on the beach. Not a kiss between friends. A kiss between two in love.

Something rustles nearby and I turn in fear. Just a

squirrel, how silly. Since when do I scare so easily? I walk by the birch tree sentries, standing post on either side of the path, past the brambleberry bushes now hanging fat with sweet-tart treasures. I part the heavy thicket of evergreen branches and now, at last I am here.

The smell of pine envelops me in perfume, like incense from the church. I breathe in and out, deeply, fully, in and out and in again. The House of Pine? A princess? Perhaps a *queen*? I shiver. How can this be true? Shocking news, but yet not so shocking. It is as if somehow I have known all along. Now the longing, the dreams, my choice . . . it all begins to make sense.

I am frightened. I hug my arms about me. What will my future be?

Gracepearl, my girl.

"Ohhh!" I cry out. "Mother, at last. So you haven't abandoned me."

I am with you always.

"Will Father live? Please tell me. Why didn't you answer me these long days in the hospital? When I needed you most, you left me alone."

Oh, Grace. . . . How to explain . . .

Mother is silent for a long while.

How can a mother ever explain what it is to be a mother. The joy of carrying a child inside your very body, then the anguish of her leaving you, replaced with the joy of now holding her wriggling in your arms. And then this precious child is with you every day, day upon day, year upon year, and you try to teach her all of the very best things you know, all the time knowing that she has more to teach you, and then, before you know it, she is birthed painfully from you once again. This child is a woman now, and you must let her go.

I let Mother's words sink into me. I try to understand. "But Mother, what of Father. Will he live?"

"Pearl!" Mackree's voice tells me he's near.

"Mackree," I call out.

And then there's his face flushed from running, framed all around with pine. He steps into the clearing. He comes and touches my arm. "Nurse said you were at home, but I knew you'd be here. Good news, Pearl! Your father awakens."

❖ ❖ ❖ ❖ ❖

"Talk of nine lives," Nurse Hartling says to Father the next morning, "why Cook, you are lucky as a cat."

Father laughs and Nurse Hartling raises her hand. "No laughing, you must rest."

"That's right, Father," I say, shaking my finger. "No laughing, no talking, no anything, just rest."

"Is that a royal order?" Father whispers to me with a wink.

"Yes," I say, "it is."

Nurse Hartling leaves. I'm so relieved. This king is a cat indeed. And, in that moment when my heart allows my head to clear, something wonderful begins to dawn upon me.

"Father!" I exclaim. "Is there a ship for the House of Pine?"

"Yes indeed, darling. I called for it last summer when I feared my end drew near."

"The thirteenth boat . . ." So that explains. "Captain Jessie?"

Father nods, smiling. "He has always been a good faithful friend of the family. Loyal and true."

Cock-a-doodle-do
The princess lost her shoe!
Her Highness hopped,
The fiddler stopped,
Not knowing what to do.

CHAPTER 29

The Summersleave Ball

I wake before dawn on the morning of the Summersleave Ball. There is no one at the beach. The sky is purple with a rising curtain of shimmering red out along the horizon. I mount the steps of the old bell tower to wait for the sun to announce the new day. The tower now makes me think of a castle. A princess.

Princess Gracepearl Cole. Who is she?

Mackree promised to keep Father's surprising birthday revelation to me a secret. I chose not to tell Lu and Nuff just yet, for as much as I love them, I wanted my mind to be clear so I could hear my own voice talking. Now I understand why Mother is more silent of late. She is teaching me to listen to myself.

Caw. A gull spreads its wings near. *Caw, caw, caw,* like a trumpeter heralding the arrival of royalty.

Yes, yes indeed, the regal sun. The sky brightens and gold rises straight up out of the sea.

I close my eyes in gratitude. Immediately the faces appear. And while I have never met even one of them, they now feel like family.

"Soon," I say. "I am coming."

✧ ✧ ✧ ✧ ✧

In the afternoon, after my kitchen duties, I gather some daisies, cornflowers, and lilybells and go to meet Lu and Nuff at Nuff's cottage to prepare for the Summersleave Ball.

We fix each other's hair. I weave a crown of wildflowers like I've worn each year since we were first old enough to go to the dances. The Muffets always ask why I'm "wearing weeds" on my head. I smile to myself. Wouldn't the Muffets be surprised if I were to wear my new crown! But, no, I have not yet decided.

"What are you smiling about, Gracie?" Lu says.

"So many things," I say. "So many things."

"Aren't you the mysterious one," Nuff says.

Nuff's mother brings in her basket of face colors, creams, and powders. She lets us each pick a favorite perfume. I choose the one that smells of pine.

And then, all at once without warning, no bells or bursts of light, I know what I must do. Something my whole self is certain of. "Till tonight!" I say, and rush off.

When I reach the beach, the gulls welcome me. The sun hangs low in the sky. I find a good driftwood stick and a smooth stretch of sand upon which to write:

I draw a heart around my words and toss the stick aside, my body trembling with excitement and hope and love.

I hurry to the cottage, find a sheet of paper, dip the quill pen into ink. I write a note to Mackree, instructing him to go to the beach before sunset, walk to the top of the bell tower, and look down. An important message awaits him. "Then meet me at the Summersleave Ball."

I run to Mackree's stable and stick the note in a prominent place by Ransom's stall. A place Mackree will most certainly see when he comes to feed the horse. Heart singing like my sea-chimes, I hurry home to dress.

✧ ✧ ✧ ✧ ✧

Lu and Nuff and I walk to the ball together. We see the torches as we approach; the faint sound of music wafts through the air. The Muffets are blocking the entrance steps, having long since claimed the prime spots to be seen by the princes in training. The Muffets don't speak to us as we pass. They aren't even speaking with each other, too busy they are straining their necks up like ostriches hoping to be the first to spot the princes and push their dance cards toward them.

My dance card is in my purse. I filled it in before I left the cottage.

Every line reads "Mackree."

❖❖❖❖❖

The royals arrive, one here, two there, Sir Blake, Sir Marcus, Sir Hickory Dickory Dock. Sir Humpty rolls in next, festooned in a light blue velvet cape, matching blue ribbons tied throughout his blond curls. Lu, Nuff, and I roll our eyes.

Lady Jule arrives with Professor Millington and Professor Quill. "Etcetera, etcetera," Nuff says. Professor Gossimer comes next, chatting with Professor Daterly. Professor Pillage walks alone. Then there's a squeal from the Muffets section as Sir Richard and Sir Peter make their appearances.

"Oh, they are gorgeous," Lu swoons. "Sir Richard looks sweeter than a whole box of sea taffy."

Madame Bella strikes the gong. "Let the music begin."

First up is a waltz. I watch the door for Mackree.

Sir Richard approaches me. "Lady Gracepearl, may I have this dance?"

"No, sir," I politely decline. I look to the door for Mackree.

"But I have something important of which to speak to you."

"Thank you, Sir Richard." I look straight into his eyes so there will be no doubt of my sincerity. "You are very kind and I am honored, but I must respectfully decline your . . . *offer.*" I need not say the word "marriage," as we both know what I mean. "You are a fine prince, indeed, but my heart is beholden to another."

"Ahh," he says, "the stable boy."

"How did you know?" I say.

"When I came awake after the accident at the tournament and saw all these faces, hovering to know my condition, I asked Sir Peter where you were. He pointed across the field. I saw your face as you cared for Mackree, and your face explained everything."

"You are a fine PIT," I say.

He laughs. "So that's what you think of me, the hard old center of a peach?"

"No," I say, laughing, "PIT stands for prince in training. My friend Lu made up the name."

"Lu," Sir Richard says. "The sweet girl of the sweet taffies."

"Sir Richard," I say. "Did you ever notice that Lu only leaves those taffies on the pillow of one particular prince?"

Sir Richard is silent for a moment and then his face lights up with recognition.

"That's right," I say.

"Go ask her to dance," I say. "Go now, quickly, before her card fills up. She is a peach, Sir Richard, a prize. You would be lucky to win her affection."

One waltz leads to another. Mackree does not come.

The princes have clearly mastered the charming art of ballroom dancing. Everyone is dancing but me. The Muffets gasp as Tattlebug makes a surprise appearance, looking very nice indeed. When I had encouraged her to come to the ball, she said she didn't have a dress. Lu offered a pale yellow gown that she'd outgrown and I brought it to Tattlebug's cottage yesterday with a pretty crimson shawl and some barrettes for her hair. I walk toward Tattle . . . Nell Tattler to tell her how nice she looks, but then I see Sir Humpty. He is smiling at Nell. She is smiling at him. She walks toward him and then they are dancing. Good for them.

Sir Peter approaches me. "Will you walk on the terrace with me, Gracepearl? There is something I want to . . ."

And as with Sir Richard, I graciously explain why

I cannot. I see Nuff at the punch bowl nearby us. "Sir Peter," I say, "do you know my friend Nuff?"

"Of course," he says. "I have wanted to speak with her more. But when we first arrived on Miramore, I asked her on a date and she declined. She said her friend Gracepearl liked me. I take it that she was mistaken?"

Oh, Nuff, dear Nuff, putting my wish for a ship before her very own heart. "I like you very much, Sir Peter," I say. "But it is another I love. Look how regal, how beautiful Nuff is. And she has humor to match yours. And Sir Peter, if you can keep a secret. She gave you five stars on the beach the first day."

"Five out of . . ."

"Five," I say, "the top rating of all."

"Really?" Sir Peter says, his face breaking into a smile.

"Yes, Sir Peter, really. Go, dance."

❖ ❖ ❖ ❖ ❖

A fast waltz begins and I take a seat in the corner looking up at the doorway at the top of the stairs, waiting for Mackree to arrive. One waltz leads to another. I smile watching Lu and Richard and Nuff and Peter and yes, even Nell Tattler and Humpty. What does she see in Humpty, I wonder. But then I see how he looks at her. He seems to find her charming. Maybe even bad eggs deserve another chance.

The night wears on. It must be nearly midnight. Oh where are you, Mackree? Why have you not come?

The flower crown itches my head now. The punch tastes warm and putrid. Where is Mackree? I watch the dancers. I watch the entrance. Waiting, waiting.

What if he never discovered the note? What if he read it and went to the beach, but the tide had washed my question away? Or, oh no, what if he read the question but the answer is . . .

Then, suddenly, he is there.

Standing on the top step looking down, Mackree turns his head to the far left side of the room, slowly scanning the dance floor until his face makes its way to me.

Our eyes lock. He smiles at me. And though the music is loud and our distance far, I can hear his answer.

"Yes."

Yes, yes, yes, yes, yes.

Old King Cole was a merry old soul,
And a merry old soul was he,
He called for his pipe,
And he called for his bowl,
And he called for his fiddlers three.

CHAPTER 30

Something More than Miramore

Mackree was late getting to the dance because after he read my message he needed to run home to wash up and have his mother press his holiday clothes. Then he went to the hospital to see Father. To ask for his blessing. A blessing joyfully bestowed.

When I told Lu and Nuff about my royal lineage, they were not totally shocked.

"It explains all those dreams," Nuff said. "And it's a much more elegant solution than trying to encourage Mackree Byre to build himself a boat!"

So that's what Nuff was doing at Mackree's. I should never have doubted either of them.

"You always were special," Lu said.

"But we are the same," I say. "This doesn't change our friendship."

"Just think, Gracie," Lu laughs, still giddy after having danced all night with Sir Richard, "all this time . . . *you* were a PIT. A *princess* in training. Imagine that!"

"Like a fairy tale," Nuff says, smiling. "A fairy tale come true."

But what will the ending be? I hear Mother's voice in my head.

❖ ❖ ❖ ❖ ❖

My Miramore friends and neighbors, the professors, and most of the PITs gather on the beach to bid me and Mackree safe journey. Captain Jessie Tru has the ship ready. The daughter of the royal one he transported to Miramore long ago now requires passage home to Pineland. "Always at service to the Order," Captain Jessie says to me.

"But what of the spiked shoals and the sucking pools of fire," I ask.

"There are no such things," Captain Jessie says. He spits and shakes his head. "Just old stories the Order contrived to keep the working classes here serving the school and the mills."

I am outraged. "You mean they were lies? That's despicable. They had no right to deceive us that way!"

Captain Jessie shrugs. "Aye. I'll have you home quicksafe, Princess."

At the word "home" my throat tightens in a knot.

Lu and Nuff wrap their arms around me, cooing words of undying friendship and love. "Enough, enough, before I lose my courage," I say, one palm on Nuff's face, the other on Lu's, shaping two arcs of a heart. "I shall return soon, I promise."

I climb up on a rock. "Listen, my friends, everyone. There are no deadly spiked shoals, no sucking fiery whirlpools."

Sounds of astonishment rise up.

"I will prove it," I say. "I will be the first to sail out past that line of horizon. And may that give you courage to follow if you so choose. This is a new age with new rules. Let your heart rule from this point forward."

"You sound like a queen already," Lu says, her dear face flushed with tears.

"Be sure that captain remembers the way back," Nuff says. "We expect you to visit soon."

"Do you want to come with us, Nuff?"

"No, Gracie. Miramore is my place. I have all I want right here."

Sir Peter steps forward. He puts his arm around Nuff. "It may be premature," he says, smiling at Nuff. "But when the ship from Elmland comes for me next month, I think I will send it off filled with fabrics alone. If it pleases Lady Nuff, I may stay on awhile."

He looks at Nuff and the smile they share says it all.

I hug Nuff and whisper, "I'm so happy for you, friend.

"Lu, what of you," I say. "Do you want to come with us?"

"I may soon be off to Ashland for a visit," she whispers. "Richard wants to show me all the fine restaurants and sweetshops."

"Oh, really, Lu?" I hug her. "How wonderful!"

I have never seen my friend look so happy.

"But listen," I say. "Promise me something. Keep your sea taffy recipe to yourself!"

Lu laughs. "I promise."

❖ ❖ ❖ ❖ ❖

Mackree lifts the purple trunk onto the boat. In it are some treasures—all the birthday gifts from Mother, a few wind chimes and sea-signs and the frayed old volume of rhymes, the history book, the satchel of papers, a purple box with a crown inside.

Tattlebug hovers in a corner.

"Good, Nell, come," I say. "I have a gift for you."

She takes it from my hands. "Your spyglass," she says, her eyes widening. "But . . ."

"I figured you might enjoy it, knowing how you like to keep an eye on things."

She laughs and hugs me. "Oh, yes, Gracepearl, thank you." She puts the spyglass to her eye and seeks out Sir Humpty in the crowd.

"Here," Nora Baker says to me. She hands me a basket filled with food for our trip and a sticky stack of papers with a slip of kitchen twine tied round.

Recipes, full of misspelled words, and full of love too.

"Someday you might wanna learn to cook," she says.

Nora looks at Captain Jessie and smiles. He hugs her awkwardly. "You're a good woman, Nora," he says.

"Get on there," she says, shooing him off. There are tears in her eyes.

I remember the night of the Welcome Banquet when I told her a mysterious thirteenth ship had arrived.

"You knew, Nora. Didn't you? All along."

"Yes." She nods.

"Why did you never say anything?"

"'Twasn't my place," she says. "I always knew my place. I served your mother and father."

"Yes you did, Nora. So very well. And you taught me much indeed. Thank you," I say, hugging her. "I will miss you."

She pulls back. "Take good care of her, ya hear me," she says to Mackree, her chin thrust up to emphasize her words and to also keep the tears from slipping out.

Oh, Mother, I call out silently. *I don't know if I can . . .*

Yes you can, Gracepearl, my girl. Mother's voice is rock

solid. *The world is your oyster. You're a pearl full of grace. You have everything you need.*

"No good-byes," Father says.

"I love you," I say, trying to be brave. What if his heart takes him from me before I can return?

"Send word when you are settled," Father says.

We hug for what seems like forever, until I feel Mackree's hand touch mine.

"Ready, Pearl?" Mackree says.

I find harbor in his eyes, those deep violet pools, and I know that indeed I am.

❖ ❖ ❖ ❖ ❖

Captain Jessie pulls up anchor. My eyes sweep every face, the flowers, the trees, the gull in the tower, every inch of Miramore. I lock them safe in the trunk of my memory.

Waves of sadness crash against waves of joy, waves of excitement topple waves of fear.

"Pearl," Mackree says.

"My heart," I say.

He hugs me, I kiss him, and the ship sets sail as our friends cast good luck flowers, whistles, and cheers from the shore. Little Leem and Brine skip stones our way, one so far it hits the hull. I raise my fist to congratulate them.

Some who play at the forest dances have brought their fiddles for the occasion.

"Let's dance," I say, and Mackree laughs.

He twirls me around and then I twirl him. We dance

and dance and dance through the mist, till I can no longer see Miramore.

I close my eyes. I see the faces. *I am coming,* I say.

I know not what the future holds.

The House of Pine, a throne or not, much is still fog before me.

One thing for certain I know right now.

I am happy.

Happily happy.

Ever after?

We shall see.

Dance to the fiddlers,
Dance to the fiddlers,
Dance to the fiddlers.
Whee!

Acknowledgments

With sincerest gratitude to:

My amazing editor, Alisha Niehaus, a particularly fine gardener, for planting the perfect seed of an idea and then giving it time to grow; my publisher, Lauri Hornik; Regina Castillo, Nancy Leo-Kelly, Lily Malcom, and all of the talented people at Dial.

My wonderful agents, Tracey and Josh Adams, for their wisdom and encouragement.

My brother Jerry for rock solid love.

My friends Pauline Kamen Miller, Kathy Johnson, Maureen Goldman, Kathi Shamlian, Ellen Donovan, Corey Jamison, Ellen Laird, Chloe Carlson, Eric Luper, Robyn Ryan, Rose Kent, Frank Doberman, Nancy Davison, Judy Calogero, Kyra Teis, Karen Beil, Mary Grace Tompkins, Ellen Snyder, Kate Sorrentino, Colleen McNulty Murtagh, Marion Hannan, and Jane Spain Ducatt for staunch support through a difficult voyage.

My son Dylan, for helping me discover *"mo chroi,"* pronounced *"muh-kree,"* means *"my heart."*

My son Chris, for patiently teaching me how to use the sunny yellow laptop that had been gathering dust in a box.

My son Connor, for asking me daily how the writing was going and for listening with interest to my answers.

My mother, Peg Spain Murtagh, for her unwavering belief in me and for a particularly heart-expanding conversation on a winter's ride back home from Old Forge, New York, where I had spoken at the Town of Webb Schools and the Old Forge Library and where my mother and I had lunch at the Van Auken Inn, where she told me my great-grandmother Grace Pearl Cole had once worked in the kitchen. At that moment a firefly sparked inside. I now had my protagonist's name.

My "peace of the planet," Cape Cod, where I wrote the first draft of this novel in the solitude of eight perfect February days. Each morning as I walked the beach, small treasures—an oyster shell, a purple ribbon, a pinecone, a whale-shaped rock—three or four things would call out to me and I would pocket them. Back at the cottage, I would set these "sea-signs" on the table, make a cup of tea, light a candle, and begin to type, fingers flashing furiously across the keyboard as my morning treasures blossomed into scenes, sometimes whole chapters, in Gracepearl's story.

My teachers at the College of Saint Rose, Albany,

New York, where I earned my bachelor of arts degree in English, particularly Sister Elizabeth Varley, Dr. Stephen Hirsch, Sister Kitty Hanley, Dr. S. R. Swaminathan, Sr. Patricia Kane, Sr. Rose Bernard, Sr. Joan Lescinski and Sr. Catherine Cavanaugh. Thanks, also, to Dr. Lynn Levo and Dr. Patricia Hayes and to Sister Nancy Burkhardt, Catholic Central High School, Troy, New York, who stared me hard in the eyes one day after our AP English class and at a difficult time when I sorely needed it, told me I was "a writer" and encouraged me to enter a national writing competition in which I later won first prize in the playwriting category. Thanks also to my fine teachers in the graduate English program at Trinity College, Hartford, Connecticut, whose names have escaped me, but not the memory of their love of literature. There is no profession nobler than that of a teacher. The seeds you plant are perennial.

Posthumously to my great-grandmother Grace Pearl Cole, whom I never met, but who through the extensive genealogical research of my aunt Virginia Spain Meyers, we have discovered was a descendant of the Mayflower Coles who trace back to the Old King Cole of nursery lore. Well, who knew?! (As my son Connor always says ☺)

Finally, thanks to my readers. I am humbled by your faith in me and grateful for your loyalty. If you enjoyed this book, please pass it along to a friend with the